FIVE FEET OF PURE WOMAN
AND SIX INCHES OF COLD STEEL

"Way I heard it," Mark said, "those fellers on the Newton bank robbery hadn't much of an idea how to handle the job. They hit the bank at evening, when there was only one teller in it. Then they only took thirty thousand, although there was nearly three times that in the vault."

"That sounds like the gang spooked, or bad management."

"I bet you could have handled it better."

Just why he said it, Mark would never know. It may have been a clumsily worded compliment, meant to show his appreciation for her ability. Or it could have been a blind flash of intuition.

A low hiss left Marigold's lips. Her right hand dipped into the vanity bag, came out with something in it. Mark felt that something boring into his side.

"How long have you known?" she asked.

"Known what?" Mark replied, looking down at the Navy Colt Marigold held like she knew which end the bullet left from.

"That I'm Belle Starr."

Other Dell Books by J. T. Edson

THE NIGHTHAWK

NO FINGER ON THE TRIGGER

THE BAD BUNCH

SLIP GUN

J. T. EDSON

TROUBLED RANGE

A DELL BOOK

Published by
Dell Publishing
a division of
Bantam Doubleday Dell
Publishing Group, Inc.
666 Fifth Avenue
New York, New York 10103

ISBN: 0-440-20773-8

Printed in the United States of America

December 1990

10   9   8   7   6   5   4   3   2   1

OPM

*For Major "Digger" Radford, R.A.V.C., Rtd.,
who had the horrible job of putting up with
me in two countries*

1

THE BOUNTY ON BELLE STARR'S SCALP

Curses crackled around Calamity Jane in a profane cloud as she stood, hands on hips, looking at the left front wheel of her wagon which had sunk through the caved-in roof of a prairie-dog hole, then slowly raised her eyes to study the setting sun.

With all the West to pick from as digging ground, trust that blasted, fool critter to sink his tunnel right in the route her wagon was taking. Of course it might be claimed that the prairie dog had been on the range first and she ought to have avoided its hole, but Calamity had never been a girl to admit she might be in the wrong.

"Dad-blast your ornery, worthless hole-grubbing hide!" she spluttered. "The hosses'll never haul it out and night's near on here. I may as well make camp and cook up a meal, so keep out of sight, prairie dog, or you'll be that meal."

Calamity Jane had reached the mature age of eighteen and already bore a name fast becoming famous. Soldiers in the Army's string of forts claimed her acquaintance. Freighters boasted of having been the one who taught her to wield a blacksnake whip. More than one dance-hall girl now knew to sing low when Calamity Jane swaggered into a saloon.

Her red hair had a natural curl to it, hung medium long,

and carried a U.S. Cavalry kepi perched on it. The face framed by the hair was pretty, freckled and tanned. A merry face with lips made for laughter or kissing, but capable of turning loose a blistering flow of invective should she be riled. Her figure had matured early and now at eighteen the breasts rose round and full. They forced hard against the dark blue Cavalry shirt, its neck opened far enough to give a tantalizing glimpse of the opening of the valley between her breasts. The shirt, like her buckskin pants, seemed to have been bought a size too small and shrunk in the wash. The pants clung tight to her hips which swelled out and down to sturdy but shapely legs with Pawnee moccasins on the feet. Round Calamity's neck hung a string of freshwater pearls, her sole concession to feminine jewelry. Her arms, exposed by the rolled up sleeves, looked more muscular than a lady of fashion might have liked. Calamity had never laid claim to being a lady of fashion, or any other kind. Nor would a lady of fashion be likely to wear a gunbelt, with a .36 Navy Colt butt forward in a fast draw holster at her right side. Calamity wore such a rig and knew how to use it.

"I'll light a fire afore I unhitch you, boys," she told her two-horse team. "Maybe somebody'll see the flames and come lend us a hand."

Collecting wood and buffalo chips from the rawhide possum belly under the wagon, Calamity built a fire. She took water from the butt on the side of the wagon, filled her coffeepot and set it to boil on the flames.

All in all, Calamity made an attractive picture as she prepared to make her camp. She attracted the attention of the rider who topped the rim behind her and halted his horse to drink in the scene below.

Sitting his seventeen-hand stallion lightly, no mean feat for a man who topped six foot three in his bare feet and had the muscular development of a Hercules, the man looked down at Calamity. He shoved back his costly white, low-crowned, wide-brimmed Stetson from his curly golden-blond hair. The blue eyes looked out of a strong, tanned, almost classically handsome face. Knotted and tight rolled at his throat, the scarlet silk bandana trailed long ends over the expensive tan shirt. He clearly bought the shirt, and all his clothing, made to his measurements. Few stores could supply clothes to fit him off their racks. His shoulders had a great spread to them, the arms showing their enormous biceps even though the shirt's sleeves had been built generously. Tapering down to a lean waist, the body rested on long powerful legs clad in jeans which hung outside his boots and had their cuffs turned back. His boots had the look of good workmanship and the gunbelt, with a matched brace of ivory-handled 1860 Army Colts in the holsters, bore the marks of a master craftsman's hands. Whoever tooled that belt knew just what a man needed in the interests of drawing his guns very fast.

The big man might look something of a dandy dresser, but he had an air of quiet self-reliance. He seemed to be at home on the range, although his home range would lie some distance to the south of Montana Territory.

A touch of the Kelly spurs on the heels of his fancy-stitched boots started his blood-bay stallion moving. Before the horse had taken five steps Calamity heard its hooves and turned, hand hovering over the butt of her gun.

"Texan," she mused, studying his hat, then the low-horned, double-girthed saddle between his knees. "Cowhand. A good 'un or I've never seen one."

Despite her thoughts, Calamity did not relax until the Texan halted his horse before her and doffed his hat in a gallant gesture, then nodded to the wagon.

"Howdy, ma'am. You-all having trouble?"

"*Naw!*" she scoffed. "I just naturally like sitting here with the wheel all bogged down and the wagon stuck. 'Course I'm not in trouble."

"That being so," he replied calmly, his voice a deep, cultured Southern drawl, "I'll be on my way again. *Adios.*"

Calamity stared at him for a moment. Then a curse ripped from her lips as he started the horse moving, setting his hat on his head once more. Her hand turned palm out, closed on the butt of her Colt and brought it from the holster. Its hammer clicked back under her thumb.

"Hold it!" she snapped. "You come back here and lend me a hand to get the wagon out, or I'll put lead into you."

Turning, the blond Texan surveyed her gun with calm

detachment. He twisted in his saddle to do so and made no attempt to turn the blood bay around.

"Say please," he answered.

"Do you know who I am?"

"No, ma'am."

"The name's Canary! Martha Jane Canary. Which, if you're so damned all-fired uneddicated, spells Calamity Jane—and means I'm Wild Bill Hickok's gal."

If Calamity expected her words, or fear of the famous Wild Bill Hickok's name to bring the Texan to a condition of servile obedience, she was to be disappointed. Tapping his Stetson to the correct "jack-deuce" angle over his off eye with the forefinger of his right hand, the Texan answered, "Which is as good a reason as any I know not to help you. I never took to Wild Bill in any size, shape or form."

Once more he started the horse moving and Calamity's temper popped right over the boiling point.

"Hold it, damn you!" she howled and fired a shot, the bullet hissing by the big Texan's head.

This time she got a reaction, although not the one she wanted. Barely had she fired when the Texan turned—only he held an Army Colt in his left hand.

Calamity had not been watching his left hand. She knew that most men only carried two guns to have twelve shots handy instead of six. The Army Colt might be one of the finest percussion-fired revolvers ever made, but it still took time to reload with combustible cartridges or powder flask and ball. Only a few men could handle the left side gun worth a damn. It was in keeping with her lousy luck that she should tie in with a jasper who not only could, but just had showed remarkable skill when using his good left hand.

Flame spurted from the Texan's Colt and dirt erupted between Calamity's feet causing her to take a hurried, if involuntary, step to the rear.

"Leather it!" snapped the Texan, cocking his gun on the recoil, "or I'll blow it out of your hand."

He could likely do it too. Calamity had not failed to notice the smooth ease with which he threw lead at the end of a very fast draw. It struck between her feet, but she was willing to bet the bullet went within an inch or two of where the big feller aimed it to go.

"Wild Bill's not going to like this," Calamity warned, twirling her Navy Colt on the trigger finger, twisting it around and thrusting it back into the holster. Her attitude was one of "that showed him how to handle a gun."

"Looking at your wagon, you won't be headed anywhere to snitch to him about me," the Texan replied.

The gun in his hand spun in a flashing arc, pinwheeled up into the air and slapped its barrel into his palm, curled around his hand like a trained pig on a barrel, rose into the air once more, was caught and went back into the holster.

Calamity stared, her eyes bulging like organ stops. Having seen a number of prominent gentlemen of the gunfighting fraternity, she felt she could speak with some authority on the new and honorable art of pistol-juggling—which was not a show-off stunt, but a method of strengthening the wrists and improving the ability to handle the weapon. One thing Calamity knew for sure. The display she had just seen equaled the best it had ever been her privilege to witness.

"What do I have to do afore you help?" she asked.

"Like I said, say please."

"Wouldn't want me to say pretty please, would you?"

"*Adios,*" drawled the Texan and started the blood bay moving.

"All right, blast you!" Calamity wailed. "Please, damn you, please!"

"Now that's a heap better," grinned the Texan, swinging his horse towards her. "World'd be a happier place if we all asked each other polite."

"I hope Wild Bill asks you polite when he blows your ears off for what you done to me!" Calamity howled.

"That'd be the only way he could do it, gal," the Texan told her as he dismounted and looked around him. "There's nothing handy we could use as a lever?"

"I saw that hours back, you danged knobhead!" gasped the infuriated Calamity. "What're you fixing to do about it?"

"Think first," answered the Texan calmly. "What'd Wild Bill do?"

"He'd lay hold of that wheel and heft the whole blasted wagon up!"

"Would, huh? Have you any more logs under the possum belly?"

Reaching into the rawhide carrier, Calamity hauled out two thick logs.

"These do?" she asked, having decided sarcasm would get her nowhere.

"Why sure. Get set to slide them in under the wheel."

"How?" she snorted. "Or are you kin to that prairie dog and aim to dig the wheel out with your paws? Some pesky varmint stole my shovel back in Hays."

"Wasn't Wild Bill there to watch it?" asked the man.

Only with an effort did Calamity prevent herself throwing the logs at the Texan. She had considerable knowledge of men, far more than a girl her age in conventional circles would have gained in a lifetime, but that Texan sure licked the bejesus out of the others when it came to riling a girl and getting her pot-boiling mad.

After waiting for some comment for a couple of seconds, the big Texan walked to the wagon. For a moment he stood looking at it, then turned his back to the trapped wheel, bent his legs slightly and gripped the spokes.

"Quit trying, feller," Calamity said. "Not even Wild Bill could lift that wagon."

The handsome blond giant did not reply. Standing with his back to the sunken wheel, he took a firmer grip and slowly put on the pressure in an attempt to raise it.

For almost thirty seconds nothing happened, except that the Texan's face showed the strain, twisted into determined lines and became soaked with sweat. Calamity opened her mouth to make some comment about the foolishness of a lesser mortal attempting something which would have been beyond the power of even the mighty Wild Bill Hickok.

Her words never came. Before her eyes the wagon began to rise, lifting a fraction of an inch at a time, but going steadily upwards. Calamity stopped thinking about Wild Bill Hickok and grabbed a log, ready to thrust it under the wheel.

"Just a lil mite higher, friend!" Calamity breathed, kneeling by his side and lowering the log into the hole. The wheel rose a couple of inches higher. "Easy now! Can you hold it?"

With his breath hissing through his teeth and every muscle and fiber of his giant frame concentrated on the effort, the Texan made no attempt to reply. But he braced himself firmer and held the wagon. He looked like he might be posing for a painting of some legendary classic hero performing a superhuman feat, like Hercules carrying out one of his labors, or Atlas limbering up to heft the world on his shoulders once more. Calamity did not have a classical education, in fact beyond being able to read slowly and write a painful, childish scrawl, her schooling had been remarkably poor. To her the big Texan sure looked a heap of man.

Not that she wasted much time in staring. Calamity was an extremely practical young woman, if hot-tempered and hotheaded. She knew there would be limits to the giant Texan's strength and that she must get the supporting log under the wheel before the wagon's weight proved too much for him.

"Lower away, friend!" she said, satisfied the log under the wheel would hold.

Slowly the Texan bent his legs, letting the weight settle down gradually, not dropping it as most men would have, not that most men could have performed the task of lifting the wagon's weight. Calamity watched it sink, biting her lip in anxiety. If the log did not hold she would be to blame, not the Texan, and she could imagine the Texan's blistering comments if she failed in her side of the business after he had succeeded so well in his.

The log held, and Calamity breathed a sigh of relief. Springing to the heads of her horses, she looked at the big Texan. He had moved away from the wagon, turned to face it and now stood with his head hanging, chest heaving as he sucked air into his lungs.

"Giddap!" she yelled, pulling on the horses' head stalls. "Come on, you no-good, slab-sided, spavined, wored-out worthless apologies for crowbait. Pull."

Throwing their weights into the harness, the two horses pulled. The wagon rolled forward, stuck for a moment as its wheel hit the rim of the hole, lurched, rose up on the rim and forward. Calamity grinned broadly. She aimed to show—

"Hold it! Throw back on those horses, you fool female!" An angry bellow left the Texan's lips and, without meaning to, Calamity obeyed the order and stopped her team. Hot and angry words bubbled inside her. She did not take to any man, even if she maybe owed him thanks for helping her out of a tricky spot, talking that way to her.

"What's eating you?" she asked, deciding to start the horses moving again and to hell with him, but not doing it until she had asked the question.

"Let's not drop the back wheel into the hole," the Texan answered dryly. "Where in hell did you learn to handle a wagon—from Wild Bill?"

"You wait, mister. You just wait!" Calamity said, but she said it under her breath for she was writhing with shame at having forgotten something the rawest cook's louse in a freighting outfit would have remembered. Being Calamity, she blamed the Texan's attitude for causing her to forget the important detail of ensuring the rear wheel did not follow its leader into the hole, miss the log and bog the wagon down again.

Stamping her feet down angrily, Calamity stormed towards the wagon and studied the hole. The Texan's warning had come just in time. Another second and the wheel would have sunk down into the hole.

Taking the second log, Calamity packed it into the hole alongside the first. Grubbing some earth from the sides, she piled it over the logs, then stood up.

"That do it?" she asked.

"Reckon it might. Give her a whirl."

The Texan's cool, relaxed attitude almost pushed Calamity to the bursting point. Turning on her heel, she threw herself at her horses' heads and gripped the nearest reins. Common sense returned the moment she touched the reins. Instead of giving the word and making the horses jerk, she eased them forward inch by inch. The wagon advanced steadily, its wheel rolling onto the logs, with Calamity Jane holding her breath, leaning to one side so she could watch it roll onto the logs.

"Keep it going easy, gal," the Texan said, also watching the wheel.

At the edge of the hole, the wheel stuck for an instant, then lifted and passed over onto solid ground. Calamity was clear of the stoppage which had delayed her. Bringing the team to a halt, she walked towards the big stranger.

"Thanks, feller," she said.

"Think nothing of it," he replied. "That coffee smells good."

"Tastes the same way. Set and rest up a spell while I unhitch my team. Then I'll cook us up a mess of vittles."

"Never could stand by and watch a lady work. So I'll just tend to my horse while you're unhitching and cooking."

While she worked, Calamity threw interested glances at her rescuer, trying to decide who he might be. One prominent Texas name fitted his appearance and strength, the way other *Tejanos* boasted about it, only that one wore his guns butt forwards for a cross-draw, or so she heard tell. This big feller's matched Army Colts were real fine weapons, with the deep blue sheen of the Hartford factory's Best Citizens' Finish; they rode in contoured holsters which hung just right, but those holsters had never been designed for cross-draw work.

After tending to his horse, the Texan walked back to the fire and laid his saddle carefully on its side. No cowhand worth his salt ever chanced damaging his rig by resting it on its skirts. Without a saddle he could do no cattle work. He set down his saddle so the butt of the Winchester Model 1866 rifle in the boot remained on top and ready for a hurried withdrawal should one be necessary.

With this done, the Texan walked across and started to help Calamity unhitch her horses. Her first inclination was to tell him she didn't need his help even though she could use it. Only she knew if she did he was likely to take her at her word and leave her to it.

"Going to say something?" he asked.

"Sure," she replied, then to hide her confusion, "I told you my name."

"Yep."

"*Yep!*"

"And now you're wanting to know mine?"

"Me! Heh!" snorted Calamity, tossing her head back in an entirely feminine manner which brought no reaction from the man. "All right then, I want to know."

"Name's Counter, my pards call me Mark."

Calamity cut down her whistle of surprise. Mark Counter. That figured, if a half-smart little range gal came to think about it.

Although his father ran a big spread down in the Texas Big Bend Country, and Mark himself had a fair-sized fortune left him by an eccentric maiden aunt in her will, he still rode as a hand for Ole Devil Hardin's O.D. Connected Ranch. More than that, he belonged to the elite of the ranch crew, the floating outfit, and was the sidekick and right bower* of the spread's segundo, the Rio Hondo gun wizard Dusty Fog. When debating to herself who Mark might be, Calamity had thought of Dusty Fog—only if Dusty Fog was bigger and stronger than Mark, it would make him a tolerable big and strong man.

During the War between the States, Mark rode as a second lieutenant in old Bushrod Sheldon's regiment where his ideas of uniform were much copied by the bloods of the Confederate Cavalry. Now Mark's taste in clothes dictated cowhand fashions in the range country, for he was an acknowledged master of the trade. His strength and ability in a roughhouse brawl were spoken of with awe by all who saw him in action. Having just seen an example of that strength, Calamity reckoned for once the Texans were not exaggerating even a little mite as they talked of this particular son of the Lone Star State. Men said Mark could handle his guns well. The few who *knew* claimed him to be second only to the man they called the fastest gun in Texas, Dusty Fog himself, in both speed and accurate placing of his shots.

"Glad to know you," she said, not wishing him to guess that she felt impressed by being in the presence of a man Wild Bill Hickok studiously avoided meeting when the O.D. Connected brought a trail herd into Hays.

Actually Wild Bill had left town on a buffalo hunt the day

---

* Right Bower, originally a euchre term for the highest trump card.

before the O.D. Connected herd arrived—he said. Calamity had taken his word for it, content to bask in Hickok's reflected glory. Only now that she came to think about it, there had been no buffalo herds seen around Hays at that time. Even the professional hunters had commented on the lack of the shaggy critters on the range.

No matter that she was hotheaded, Calamity could cook up a meal fit to set a man's mouth to watering. One of the few things the nuns at the St. Louis convent—where Calamity's mother left her children before disappearing into the unknown—had managed to teach the girl was how to cook.

They ate their meal without much talk. Then, after cleaning up the dishes, Calamity walked to where her guest stood. She reckoned it was high time they had a showdown and learned who was boss around the campfire.

"You sure cook good, Calamity," he said, grinning down at her. "Don't tell me Wild Bill taught you?"

"I'm Wild Bill's gal," she replied and whipped the flat of her hand across his cheek with all her strength.

It was a good slap, Calamity admitted to herself, maybe even a little harder than she ought—

Mark's hands shot out, clamping on her shoulders and jerking her forward. He bent his head and his lips crushed down on hers. With a muffled gasp, Calamity tried to twist her head away. Her hard little fists beat at his shoulders, but Mark ignored them. Twisting his body, he took her knee on his thigh as it drove up. Then he released her, shoving her backwards. For a moment Calamity stood gasping for breath. Then she came forward with another slap and a repetition of the fiction that she was Wild Bill's girl.

Again Mark caught her, hauled her to him and crushed a kiss on her lips. She struggled, though not as hard as before. On being released, she staggered a pace or so to the rear and stood gasping for breath.

"I'm Wild Bill's gal!" she said, her breasts heaving, and she lashed out another slap, only it did not have the power of the first two.

On the fourth, fifth and sixth kisses and slaps Calamity's

struggles grew weaker. The slaps became more feeble and on the sixth time she found herself starting to kiss back.

"I—I'm st—still W—Wild Bill's g—gal!" she gasped after the seventh kiss, staggering on wobbly legs and landing a slap which barely touched his cheek.

Once more Mark scooped her into his arms. This time her lips sought his, hungrily answering the kiss. Her tongue crept through his lips. Her arms, no longer flailing, crept around him. Clinging to Mark, her fingers digging into the hard muscles of his back, Calamity threw all she had into her kiss.

The night was dark. The stars shone brightly in the heavens. Only the range noises broke the silence; the stamping of Mark's big stallion as it heard the distant scream of a cougar; the thrashing as one of Calamity's team horses rolled in the grass; the squeaking of insects.

Under the wagon a large black mound separated into two smaller black mounds. A masculine voice spoke from the larger of the mounds.

"What do you think of Wild Bill Hickok now?" it asked.

A feminine voice, dreamy, satisfied and contented came from the smaller.

"Wild Bill Hickok," it said. "Who *is* Wild Bill Hickok?"

The sun crept up and peeped over the horizon. A cold gray light of dawn began to creep out into the blackness of the night sky.

Beneath Calamity's wagon, Mark Counter opened his eyes and lifted his head from the pillow he always carried in his bedroll. Beside him, the girl stirred sleepily, her bare arm around his equally bare shoulders. Putting up his hand, Mark felt at the oval lump on the right side of his neck. Well, the bandana would hide it and he reckoned he was big enough to handle any adverse comments on his honorable wounds.

Two arms closed around his neck and a hot little mouth crushed against his, worked across his cheek and to his ear.

"Mark!" Calamity breathed into his ear.

"It's time we was up and on our way," he replied.

"Please—pretty please."

Like the man said, a feller's sins always bounced right

back onto his fool head if he stayed around long enough after committing them; and Mark *had* taken a firm stand on the subject of politeness bringing its own reward when he first met Calamity.

Half an hour later Mark sat pulling on his boots and at his side, smiling contentedly, Calamity buttoned her shirt after tucking it into her pants.

"Yes sir," she sighed, rising to make the fire. "World's sure a happier place when we all ask each other polite."

There had been a time, back the first time it happened, when Calamity would have expected the man to marry her and spend the rest of his days in a haze of devotion to her.

Only he had not. The feller had been a handsome young freighter and Calamity a naïve sixteen-year-old girl fresh out in the harsh, cruel world. When she woke the morning after it happened, she found him gone and felt that her heart would break. It did not. Fact being Calamity had discovered her heart could stand plenty of jolting around without showing any signs of fracture. From the first time, she built up the belief that no man was so much better than the rest that he was worth busting a gut over when he pulled up his stakes and left. There would be another feller come along, so she went her own way, enjoying life to the full in good times and bad. Only she no longer grew starry-eyed when a man showed appreciation of her feminine charms.

Sure, last night had been swell, but that did not make her a potential Mrs. Mark Counter. Likely they would part in Elkhorn City and never meet again. Although she had never heard the word, would not have understood it if she did, or know how to phrase it, Calamity figured their destinies lay in different directions. While last night had been an enjoyable experience, and one she would not soon forget, nothing serious could come of it.

So Calamity cooked breakfast, while Mark used some of the contents of her water butt for his wash and shave. They ate their food with a good appetite and prepared to move on. After saddling his blood bay, Mark helped Calamity to hitch up her team to the wagon. When all was done Mark mounted his horse and Calamity swung up onto the box of her wagon, taking up the blacksnake whip.

"Giddap!" Calamity yelled, swinging her whip and making it pop like a gunshot in the morning air.

The two horses put their shoulders to the harness and moved forward, starting the wagon rolling. Side by side Calamity and Mark headed across the range, following the faint wheel ruts which marked the way to their respective business affairs in Elkhorn City.

"How come Cap'n Fog's not along with you, Mark?" she asked.

"Had some business to attend to in town and couldn't leave. Then he got this telegraph wire from a feller up in Elkhorn wanting to pay off some money he owed Ole Devil. Sent me along to collect it."

"I'd sure like to have met Cap'n Fog. How come he took his herd to Newton, not Hays, this year?"

"Saved two days driving, brought in the first drive of the year. If the railroad keeps pointing the way it is, we'll likely be delivering to somewheres around Fort Dodge next summer. You figure Wild Bill scared us off?"

"Like I said last night. Who's Wild Bill?" she grinned. "Sure would like to see Cap'n Fog though. Is all I hear about him true?"

"Such as?"

"How he stands taller'n you, is stronger, faster with his guns."

"Would you believe me if I told you Dusty Fog stands only about five foot at most?"

"Nope—hey, you're not jobbing me. You're serious, aren't you?"

Mark nodded his head. When he said Dusty Fog stood only five foot six, he told the simple truth—but to Mark's way of thinking, and to many others with whom he came in contact, Dusty Fog could not be measured in mere feet and inches, he stood the tallest of them all.

"I allus heard—!" Calamity began.

"Sure," Mark interrupted. "I've heard it too."

For a time they traveled on discussing Dusty Fog, the Ysabel Kid and the other well-known members of the O.D. Connected. Then Calamity swung the conversation to an item of news which had been the main topic in Newton during Mark's visit.

"Did you hear anything new about the bank holdup that Belle Starr's gang pulled in Newton?" she asked.

"Belle Starr's gang!" Mark snorted. "Just 'cause some old biddy who had been swigging corn whisky reckoned she saw a woman holding the gang's horses, everybody's howling about Belle Starr."

"You reckon it wasn't her then?"

"No more her than Big and Lil Harpe and they've been dead for over a hundred years."

"They put a tolerable-size bounty on her head though," Calamity replied. "It happened near on a month back, remember. Sheriff's posse run down the four fellers who pulled the raid, plumb shot them to doll rags and killed 'em all. Which came out to be plumb foolish 'cause they hadn't the money with 'em, not so much as a red cent, and they was all past telling where it'd gone."

"Yes," Mark agreed. "And now every durned fool in the West allows Belle Starr knows where the money's hid out and are looking for her to make her tell."

"Kind of like to meet her myself," remarked Calamity.

"Never took you for a bounty hunter, Calam," Mark answered, a hint of disapproval in his voice.

"And I ain't one. But they do say she's a real tough gal. I'd like to see just how tough she is."

"From Missouri, huh?"

"Huh?" Calamity replied, putting a world of puzzlement into the grunt.

"You've got to be shown."

"I've never met the gal who could lick me at riding, drinking, shooting or going at it tooth 'n' claw," Calamity stated, trying to sound modest. "And I don't reckon I ever will."

Calamity did meet a woman who was more than her match, but the meeting was not to come for three years.*

"Not interested in getting your hands on the reward the bank has offered for the recovery of the money?" asked Mark.

"Naw. Anyways, I go with you, I don't reckon Belle Starr was tied in with that raid. Hell, I know the sheriff in New-

---

* Told in *The Wildcats* by J. T. Edson.

ton, he couldn't catch water in his hat if he stood under a
waterfall. He wouldn't have picked those boys up so easy
had Belle Starr been running them."

"What brings you up this way?" Mark asked.

"Load of freight for a spread half a day past Elkhorn.
Owner had it shipped into Hays from the east and I caught
the contract to deliver it. What's this Elkhorn City like?
I've never been this way afore."

"Nor me. But they do say it's thriving, growing big and
fast, what with gold miners, ranchers and all."

"Are you fixing to be there for long?" she inquired.

"Day, couple of days at most, depends on how soon I get
to see that feller for Ole Devil."

"I'll maybe see you on my way back then," she suggested. "We can have us a wingding and paint the town a
mite."

The town known as Elkhorn City was, as Mark claimed,
growing big and fast. It sported no less than four thriving
saloons, including the Crystal Palace, a place which would
not have disgraced the best part of Trail Street, Hays City,
or the better part of any railroad trail-end town. One good
and a couple of indifferent hotels catered to the needs of
transient visitors. Various shops which usually found combination in a general store in smaller, less prosperous towns
graced Beidler Street—called after John X. Beidler, leader
of the vigilantes who wiped out the Plummer gang which
once terrorized the Bannack area. Wells Fargo maintained
a large office, stage route and telegraph service, testifying
to the importance of the city. Further amenities showed
high standards. A stout building housed the county offices,
sheriff's department, town marshal's premises and a sub-
stantial jail. In addition the town had the usual run of livery
barns, undertaker's shop and stable, bathhouse and all the
rest of the things which made life worth living on the
range.

Bringing his horse to a halt before the open double doors
of a large building inscribed POP LARKIN'S LIVERY BARN.
USE IT, I'M TOO OLD TO START WORKING, Mark looked at
Calamity, winked and raised his hat. She waved a hand,
keeping her team going forward.

"Don't you forget now!" she called. "You got a date when I come back."

Swinging from the saddle, Mark watched Calamity's wagon roll on along the street, then turned and led the blood bay towards the open doors. He did not know if he would be in town when Calamity returned, but felt tempted to stay over. Something told him a night on the town with Calamity Jane would be worth having and be a highly entertaining experience, more so since he missed most of the fun at Newton by coming north to handle the chore for Dusty Fog.

Inside the barn it was cool, light and clean looking. There were a couple of empty stalls at the end of the line across the room and Mark walked towards them, his horse following on his heels.

A man had just finished tending to his horse in a stall down the other end of the line. Turning slowly, he looked Mark over, staring at his gunbelt, dropping his eyes to the high-heeled, fancy stitched boots, then roaming them up to the top of Mark's head. Mark noticed the way the man looked, like a rancher studying a prime bull and wondering if it would bring any profit to him should he buy it.

For his part, Mark gave the man a quick, all-embracing glance and did not like what he saw. The man stood around six foot, had a lean, rangy build and a gaunt face stuck on a neck with a prominent Adam's apple. The face's expression seemed to be one of arrogant contempt, and hinted that he must be able to handle any objections to his attitude should they be made. His clothes told a story to eyes which knew the West. Sure he wore a Stetson hat, bandana, calfskin vest shirt, and jeans with their cuffs turned back, like a cowhand. He wore a gunbelt with a brace of walnut-handled Army Colts in fast-draw holsters, but so did many cowhands. On his feet were Sioux moccasins. That was what made him different. No cowhand ever wore moccasins, they would be of no use to him in his work.

For a long moment the man studied Mark, then, in the manner of a rancher who had decided a prime bull would not bring him any profit, he turned away. Slinging the saddle over his shoulder with his right hand, the man took up the double-barreled, ten-gauge shotgun which leaned against the wall of the stall. Gripping it with his left hand closed on the small of the butt, forefinger lying alongside the trigger guard, the man walked out and kicked the stall gate closed behind him.

Without appearing to, Mark watched the man walk out of the barn. Caution paid when a hardcase like that feller prowled around holding a scatter gun in his hand. The man did not look back, but walked out into the street and started across its wheel-rutted width.

"Ain't sorry to see him leave."

The words came from a door at the side of the building. Turning, Mark saw a leathery old-timer stumping towards him.

"You know him?" the old-timer went on.

"Nope. Should I?"

"Not less'n you got a wanted poster on ye some place. And you ain't, or likely one of you'd be dead by now. That there was Jubal Framant, mister."

"Is, huh?"

Once more Mark turned to look after the hardcase. He stood on the far side of the street, talking with a big, burly man who wore a marshal's shield on his vest and carried a heavy old Colt Dragoon hung low at his right side. Mark did not look down on a man who carried one of the old four-pound one-ounce thumb-busting Colt giants. The Ysabel Kid toted one and could handle it with some precision when needed.

"Yes, sir. That's Framant," the old-timer went on, following Mark's gaze. "Wonder what brings him to Elkhorn?"

"There's only one thing takes him anyplace," Mark replied.

Framant's name was not unfamiliar to Mark. The man was a bounty hunter, said to be as mean as a stick-teased rattlesnake. Roaming the range country like a buzzard circling in the sky, Framant hunted down men for a price on their heads. Rumor had it that Framant had killed fourteen men and claimed the bounty their scalps bore.

A man like Framant usually came to a town for the purpose of finding some wanted outlaw. When he found his man he would kill, for Framant never took in a living prisoner.

"Who's the feller with him?" Mark asked.

"Joel Stocker, town marshal. Real nice feller," replied the old man and turned his attention to the blood-bay stallion. "R over C. I never saw that brand afore."

"Nope?"

"Know every danged brand within five hundred miles."

"Maybe the R over C's five hundred and one miles away."

A cackle left the old-timer's lips. "Must've moved South Texas north a helluva ways if that's how close the R over C is."

"It's Rance Counter's spread."

"Tall feller, that Rance Counter, so they say. Likely sire tolerable tall sons."

"I'm the little one of the family."

"Mark Counter, huh? Pleased to know you. Pop Larkin's the name. I keep this place, leastways, it don't keep me."

"You look right poorly done by," Mark drawled, following his horse into the stall. "Wonder what Framant wants here?"

"I asked you first, and it ain't what he wants, it's who."

Mark turned to his horse and started to remove the saddle. A shadow fell across the doorway and feet crossed the barn to halt behind Mark at the gate of the stall.

"Howdy, mister," a gentle voice drawled.

For a big man Joel Stocker moved light on his feet, Mark thought, turning to look at the marshal as he leaned a shoulder against the stall's gatepost and chewed in meditative manner on a plug of tobacco. There was a deceptive lethargy about the marshal which might have fooled some folks, but not Mark Counter.

"Howdy," Mark replied, continuing the off-saddling.

"New around here?"

"Only just now rolled in."

"With Calamity Jane?"

"Sure."

"She's Wild Bill Hickok's gal, way I heard it."

"Has Wild Bill heard it?" Mark drawled.

"Don't reckon it'd scare you none if he had," Stocker replied in his sleepy voice. "It'd worry me some, though. I'm a duly appointed officer of the law and duty-bound to keep the peace. Which means I don't want no bulls locking horns in my town."

"Reckon Calam and me's just passing acquaintances. We met on the trail in and I'll likely see her tomorrow—if I'm still here then."

"Might not be, huh?"

"Not if I see Tom Gamble."

The look of watchful suspicion left Stocker's face. Straightening up, he held out a big hand and raised his eyes a couple of inches to meet Mark's, something he rarely needed to do with any man.

"Sorry, friend," Stocker said. "Reckon Framant being in town's got me spooked up a mite. Are you Cap'n Fog?"

"Mark Counter."

"Jeez! If Cap'n Fog's got more heft than you, he's a tolerable tall gent."

Mark let the remark pass. He felt no resentment at the words and it had been many years since he last felt surprised that anybody should mistake him for Dusty Fog, or persist in thinking of Dusty as a tall man. Maybe what caused the confusion was Mark looking like the kind of man one expected somebody of Dusty Fog's reputation to be. Mark did not know if this was true, and was not worried.

"Do you always look your visitors over like this?" he asked.

"Find it saves fuss to know who-all's in town," Stocker replied. "And I'm a man who likes to save fuss. There's some less welcome here than others."

"Like that bounty hunting Jubal Framant, heh, Joel?" asked the old-timer. "Are ye running him out of town?"

"Nope. I ain't saying I'm not doing it 'cause he scares me, even if he do. But he's got his rights under the Constitution —and knows 'em. I can't run a man out of town just 'cause I don't like his line of work."

While the men talked, Mark tended to his horse. He removed the saddle and bridle, then hung a hayrack on the hook over the manger. Larkin ambled off to return carrying a bucket of clean water and another full of grain. Showing sound horse savvy, he did not enter the stall, but handed the buckets over the gate.

"Got me a burro in the back if you'd like to leave your saddle," he said.

"Thanks, I'll do that. Thought you didn't have one when I saw Framant tote his rig out of here."

"There's them who I'd let use me burro, and them I wouldn't," grunted the old man. "Tote her this way."

Following the old man, Mark entered the storeroom at the rear of the stable and hung his saddle on the inverted V-shaped wooden rack known as a burro. If possible a cowhand would rather leave his saddle on a burro than lie it on its side, especially when among people which brought the danger of some heavy-footed yahoo stomping on the laid-aside rig.

Mark took his bedroll from behind the cantle and the rifle from the saddlebag. Not that he mistrusted the owner of the barn, but his change of clothing, spare ammunition and toilet articles lay in his war bag within the bedroll; and a man did not leave a loaded rifle in a saddlebag where kids might get at it.

After paying for the stabling and keep of his stallion, Mark joined Marshal Stocker at the door of the barn.

"Which's the best hotel in town?" he asked.

"Ryan's Bella Union down there, right next to the Crystal Palace. Say, Tom bust a leg riding a bad one. Sent word down that somebody from the O.D. Connected'd be along and for them to ride out and see him."

"How far out is it?"

"Two, three hours' steady ride. Could make it by nightfall."

Mark grinned. "I'll leave it until morning. What's the Crystal Palace like? Speaking as a duly appointed officer of the law, that is."

"Fair place, well-run, got some purty gals in there, and you'll walk out with any money you don't spend, or lose trying to lick the blackjack game."

"My mammy told me never to buck the dealer's percentage at any game, especially blackjack."

"It's not the game you buck in there, it's the dealer."

"What makes him so special?" Mark inquired.

"Being a her," grinned Stocker. "And a mighty purty lil

her too. Was I not a married man, which I ain't, I'd sure like
to stake a few myself on beating her game."

"As good as that, huh?" drawled Mark, ignoring the left-
handed statement made by the marshal.

"Better. Not the kind you'd expect to find working a
table even in a decent saloon like the Palace."

"They never are. See you, Marshal."

"I'll be around," Stocker answered and slouched away,
looking like he was about to fall asleep on his feet.

Mark booked a room at the Bella Union hotel and a boy
in a fancy bellhop's uniform shot forward to grab his bedroll. The boy escorted Mark up to his room, frank hero
worship plain on his face as he lugged the heavy bedroll.

On seeing his room, Mark decided it would be worth the
money. The bed had a comforting thickness and would lick
using the world for a mattress and sky for a roof. For the
rest of the furnishing, the room had a table and two chairs,
a clothes closet with a key in its door, a washstand that had
a large pitcher of water on top and a couple of clean white
towels hanging on its rail.

Tossing the boy a coin, Mark told him to find a shoeshine
man if the town had one. The youngster replied that he
doubled in shoe cleaning and said he would be back as soon
as he got rid of his dad-blasted, consarned monkey suit the
boss made him wear.

Mark took a bath in the hotel's private bathhouse, had his
hair trimmed, a barber's shave, changed his clothes, ate a
good meal and then rested in his room until after dark.
From the noise outside, he judged the town had woken up
and begun to howl, so he rose from his bed, doused the
light, put on his hat and gunbelt, then headed from the
hotel, making for the Crystal Palace.

The girl caught Mark's eye as soon as he entered the
saloon. Not because she had blond hair that curled its ends
under neatly and framed a truly beautiful face, for there
were three other blondes almost as beautiful among the
female workers of the saloon. Nor was it because she wore a
daring and revealing costume. Compared with the others
she looked demure and modest, for she did not wear the
glistening, knee-long red, green, yellow, blue or other
shade of dresses which clad the others, cut low on the

bosom and leaving, apart from the supporting straps, the shoulders and arms bare. Her white blouse had full-length sleeves, a frilly front and buttoned up to the neck. Although it tried, the blouse could not hide the rich fullness of her breasts or the slim waist, any more than the shoe-length plain black skirt concealed the fact that under it lay richly curving hips and shapely legs. Her attitude did not draw attention to her. Unlike the other girls she did not pass among the customers, laughing, joking and making herself pleasant. Standing at the busy blackjack table, she looked calmly detached, smiling at one of the players and yet not offering him any come-on encouragement.

Yet, of all the girls in the room, she took Mark's eye the moment he entered. Any way a man looked at her, she was one of the most beautiful women he had ever seen; five foot seven of undiluted voluptuous femininity trying to hide itself under those plain clothes.

For a moment Mark thought of crossing to the table and trying his luck—with the cards, not the dealer. He decided to take a drink first. If the liquor should be in keeping with the rest of the furnishings and equipment of the room, it would satisfy even the most discriminating taste.

At the bar Mark ordered a whisky, ignoring the invitation flashed in his direction by one of the girls. The drink proved to be mellow, of good standard and in keeping with the look of the saloon. From all appearances, the owners had put plenty of money into the furnishing, equipping and stocking of the place. Mark hoped the town stayed booming long enough for them to show a profit. From the look of the crowd inside, they would likely make it.

A long board, nailed to the wall opposite the main bat-wing doors, attracted Mark's attention, so he strolled over to examine it more closely. Reward posters were thumb-tacked to the board and the central sheet caught his eye.

WANTED
$5,000 REWARD
ALIVE ONLY
BELLE STARR.

There followed a drawing of a beautiful woman with shoulder length black hair framing her face, a Stetson hat perched on the back of her head, and a tight rolled bandana knotted at her throat. Beneath this followed a brief description. Mark wondered how accurate the drawing and description were, for he doubted if Belle Starr had ever been captured to be measured or sketched and nobody was likely to do it while she stayed free.

Under Belle Starr's name on the poster, and over the drawing, somebody had scrawled the words, "The Toughest Gal in the West" in a sprawling hand. Mark grinned as he read the comment, wondering what Calamity Jane would say when, or if, she read it.

As he turned away from the board, Mark became aware of somebody watching him. His instincts told him at least two sets of eyes, one on either side, studied him with more than casual interest.

To Mark's right, seated alone and ignored even by the girls paid to entertain the guests, Jubal Framant, the bounty hunter, dropped his eyes towards his whisky glass as Mark glanced in his direction. The watcher at the left appeared to be one of a quartet of scrubby-jawed, gun-hung hardcases who wore cowhand clothes but who, in Mark's considered opinion, had never worked cattle—at least not for their legal owner. On seeing Mark turn towards them, the four men resumed their drinking and talking.

Wondering a little at their interest, and not attributing it to admiration of his upstanding, manly figure, Mark walked on. He had not failed to notice that Framant had the ten gauge lying on the table before him and wondered if the man always carried the gun with him.

Putting aside thoughts of Framant's habits, Mark headed for the blackjack table. Before he reached it, Mark saw the blonde signal and a man wearing a dealer's eyeshade, white shirt, black open vest and black pants, crossed the room to take over her seat. Giving the players a dazzling smile, the blonde crossed the room towards where a door led out to the alley between the saloon and the hotel, and a flight of stairs rose to the upper part of the building.

Mark watched her go, then he saw the four hardcases

also watching. As the blonde approached the side door, one of the quartet thrust himself up, but sank back into his chair as she walked by the door and up the stairs.

Interest in the blackjack game waned and the swarm of players faded away to leave only a handful of devotees around the table. Mark himself lost his desire to sit in on the game, and strolled over to the chuck-a-luck table where he won three dollars, took them and lost them at faro. Approaching the poker game at one of the high-stake tables, he studied the play for a time. For all he could see the game, like the others, was run fairly and the house relied only on the percentage to show them a profit.

Sitting in on the poker game, Mark played until nine o'clock. He held his own even though the company consisted of talented players, for Mark was no mean hand at the art of poker.

The blonde came into sight at exactly nine o'clock and walked down the stairs. Shoving the pile of chips to the cashier of the game, Mark told the other players he was finished. A man wearing the dress of a professional gambler gave a grin, for he had seen the direction Mark looked before making the decision.

"How can the simplicity and crudity of blackjack appeal to a man of refinement when he could have the pleasure of our company, the fascination of mathematical studies and the employment of the art of bluffing while playing poker?"

"Well, I'll tell you," Mark replied to the gambler's flow of rhetoric. "If you gents looked like that blackjack dealer, I'd stay on."

"Philistine," sighed the gambler. "Meaning no disrespect, sir. My dear mother always told me never to make unfavorable comments about a man as big as you, and I believe her words. But you'll never get rich playing blackjack."

"Who wants to get rich?"

"The poor people do," the gambler replied. "Good luck with Miss Marigold Tremayne, sir. In every way."

"I might even need it," Mark replied, picking up the money the cashier passed to him. "My apologies for leaving, gents."

Crossing the room, Mark halted at a vacant place by the blackjack table and looked down at the familiar layout with the legend BLACKJACK PAYS 3 TO 2. DEALER MUST STAND ON 16 AND DRAW TO 17; followed by a list of bonuses which could be won by holding various combinations of cards which added up to no more than twenty-one; and finally came the warning, "ALL TIES STAND OFF ", meaning that if the dealer and the player held the same score on their cards the bet did not count.

"What's your limit, ma'am?" he asked, buying a stack of chips and thrusting his wallet back into the pocket built on the inside of his shirt.

"Twenty-five cents to twenty-five dollars, sir," she replied. "This-all's a friendly little game."

Her voice held a gentle Southern drawl which conjured up a hint of blooming magnolias, mint juleps on the lawn of some plantation mansion and colored folks singing their plaintive songs.

"You-all from the South?" Mark asked.

"From Memphis. And you?"

"Texas, ma'am. Or may I call you Miss Tremayne?"

"Feel free," she said, flipping the cards out to the seven men fortunate enough to get seats. "Make your bets, gentlemen."

A couple of saloon men moved in to take seats on either side of Marigold, acting as her lookouts and payoff hands. Not only would the seven men be playing, but the kibitzers and onlookers could join in, betting on the players' hands although having no say in the way the hands were played.

Watching the girl's hands flip out the cards, Mark could see no hint that she might be trying to manipulate matters in her favor. Her fingers were innocent of rings which might have tiny mirrors attached, through which she could see the value of each card as she dealt, or a spike with which to mark the cards during play. A black satin vanity bag stood on the table by her right hand, it looked a trifle larger than a lady usually carried and its jaws were open.

For a time Mark played, winning a couple of dollars, losing a couple. A plump, attractive brunette came to his side and slipped an arm around his neck, leaning on him.

"Let me bring you some luck, handsome," she suggested.

Then she straightened up and Mark opened his mouth to say something. An icy voice, still retaining its Southern drawl, but losing all visions of magnolia, mint juleps and singing, cracked from across the table.

"Hand it back, Lily!"

The brunette took a pace away from the table, eyes flashing angrily. She looked straight at Marigold and spat out, "What's eating you, sister?"

"The gentleman's wallet, Lily," Marigold answered, coming around the table and standing facing the saloon girl. "Just hand it back, and stay away from my game in the future."

"Yeah?" Lily sneered, bristling like an alley cat and curving her fingers so the nails stuck out like claws. "You go to hell, you Sou—"

Without giving the slightest warning of what she meant to do, Marigold folded her right hand into a fist and lashed it around, driving the knuckles upwards underneath Lily's jaw. Lily's mouth snapped shut with an audible click that ended her speech abruptly. She might have considered herself fortunate that her tongue had not been between her teeth when the blow landed, but Lily was in no condition to consider anything other than stars and flashing lights around her head.

Following Lily up as the brunette shot back and landed with a thud on her rump, Marigold bent down. She gripped Lily's ankles and lifted upwards, standing the tubby girl on her brunette head. Jiggling Lily, causing her skirt hem to slide down and expose a pair of shapely, black stocking-clad legs to view, Marigold shook the wallet from the bosom of Lily's frock. Thrusting Lily's legs away from her so the brunette landed on the floor once more, Marigold bent and picked the wallet up.

"I apologize for this, sir," she said, returning the wallet to Mark. "The owner and the floor manager don't allow the girls to steal wallets from the customers. Lily only started here this afternoon and doesn't know the ropes yet."

"I felt it go," Mark admitted. "But I reckon I might have had a mite more trouble getting it back than you did."

"The feminine touch can work wonders," smiled Marigold, her voice returning to how it sounded before speaking to Lily. "Shall we continue the game?"

The game resumed to admiring grins and congratulations. Mark watched the girl called Marigold Tremayne with more interest for he guessed she was not all she first appeared to be. Behind them, the floor manager helped a whimpering, jaw-nursing Lily to her feet and warned her that any further pocket-picking would see her looking for another saloon where her talents would be more appreciated. She limped away, rubbing her rump and glaring over her shoulder at Marigold.

After returning his wallet, Marigold gave no sign that Mark was any more important to her than the other players. She laughed at his comments, but no more than at the other men's remarks around the table. Her attitude set the players at ease and even the losers did not seem to care about their losses.

At half past ten Marigold folded the cards and slid them into their box. She smiled at the players and waved aside their objections to the game ending.

"Why, gentlemen," she said in a voice that would charm a bird out of a tree. "You wouldn't want a lady to miss her beauty sleep, now would you?"

From the way they looked at her, if she asked them every man at the table would have stood guard around her hotel room to make sure nobody disturbed her rest and would have counted the task an honor to perform.

Leaving the men to cash in the chips and fold up the game, Marigold swept across the room and upstairs. Mark took his money and walked across the floor to the bar. He noticed that Framant still sat alone and was watching Marigold ascend the stairs. Thinking of Framant caused Mark to look for the four hardcases, but they had left their table and did not appear to be in the big room.

Just as Mark ordered a drink, he saw one of the men reflected in the bar mirror. The man stood on the sidewalk before the main batwing doors, watching the inside of the saloon. He seemed to be looking for something and Mark wondered what, or who, that something might be.

Mark did not overlook the possibility that the man and

his pards had decided that he, Mark, might be a profitable target for a robbery. If they felt that way, Mark reckoned they would be welcome to every red cent, or whatever else they got.

For almost fifteen minutes nothing happened. The man remained outside, never looking in Mark's direction. Mark noticed this, he also became aware that the man's eyes never left the right side of the room. Suddenly the man stiffened like a bird dog catching quail scent. Turning, he walked off to the right, disappearing from the reflection in the mirror.

Looking in the direction which appeared to have interested the man, Mark saw Marigold coming down the stairs. She wore a wide brimmed, fancy-looking hat, had a shawl draped around her shoulders and carried the vanity bag hanging from her arm.

Then Mark remembered the way the hardcases reacted when Marigold crossed the room towards the stairs earlier in the evening. Finishing his drink, Mark strolled across the room and out of the main doors. He glanced back to see Marigold wave a hand to the patrons of the saloon, then open the side door and pass through it into the alley beyond.

A muffled gasp, a startled exclamation, a thud and an angry, pain-filled yelp came to Mark's ears as he approached the alley which separated the saloon from the hotel. Swinging around the corner, Mark saw two of the hardcases gripping Marigold by the arms and trying to drag her towards the rear of the building. The third man hopped on one leg, nursing his other shin and mouthing curses.

That accounted for three of the quartet. The fourth man ought to be—

Mark side-stepped fast, twisting his body and ducking his head forward. He heard the hiss as something whistled down behind him. Not expecting to miss with his gun butt's blow, the fourth man lost his balance and stumbled forward with a startled curse. He found himself headed straight for the big Texan's back. Mark drove his elbow behind him, feeling it ram into the man's middle. To the man on the receiving end of the elbow it felt as if he had

been kicked in the belly by a mule. Letting out a croak of
agony, he staggered back a few steps holding his stomach
and gasping.

The third man saw Mark avoid the blow, deal with their
lookout and head in his direction; releasing his injured
shin, but still bending forward, he hurled himself at Mark,
ramming his head into the big Texan's stomach. Mark
grunted, went back a couple of steps under the impact,
then he bent, locking his arms around the man's body from
above. Straightening up, Mark hoisted the man into the air
and landed him, with legs kicking futilely, on a broad shoulder. For a moment Mark held the man, then bent his
knees, straightened them and pitched the man over to
smash into the hotel wall from where he collapsed in a limp
pile on the ground.

A hand caught Mark's shoulder from behind and
dragged him around. The fourth man had not been so
badly hurt as Mark imagined for he completed the turn
and smashed a fist against the side of Mark's jaw, sending
him sprawling into the wall of the saloon. While the man
threw a good punch, he lacked science, which was a bad
deficiency when dealing with a fighter of Mark's capabilities.

Hitting the wall with his shoulders, Mark braced himself.
He wondered why Marigold was so quiet. By all rules of
feminine conduct she ought to be screeching her head off,
screaming for help. Yet she had not made a sound, apart
from that gasp and the hissing of her breath as she struggled with the two men holding her arms.

However, Mark did not have time to give much thought
to Marigold's silence. His braced legs held him erect and he
thrust himself forward to meet the attack of the fourth
man.

Throwing up his right hand, Mark deflected the man's
wild, unscientific blow over his shoulder. Almost in the
same movement, Mark launched his left fist viciously into
the same spot where his elbow hit earlier in the fight. The
man let out a squawk of agony, folded over and presented
his jaw to Mark's right hand blow, which ripped up at it like
iron filings to a magnet. Lifted erect by Mark's right hand,

the man stood open and asking for a left cross to finish him completely.

Mark did not have time to throw the blow, although it would not be necessary for the man was already going down. The sound of footsteps coming at his back caught his ears. He took it to mean one of the men holding Marigold had left her to his pard and moved in to the attack.

This was only partly true. One of the men had released Marigold, swung in Mark's direction and dropped his hand to his gun butt. The girl's foot came up, rested against his rump and thrust hard. Taken by surprise, both by the push and the strength Marigold showed, the man staggered towards Mark, his gun falling from his hand.

Turning fast, Mark shot out his right hand, catching the staggering man at the side of his jaw and propelling him head first into the side door of the saloon. From the limp way the man collapsed, Mark knew he had no more worries in that direction and could concentrate on dealing with the last member of the quartet.

Swinging around, Mark prepared to move forward but saw that Marigold had the situation well in hand.

After shoving the man towards Mark, Marigold turned her attentions to the other hardcase who still stood holding her right arm. Before the man knew what to expect, Marigold launched a kick against the man's shins. He yelped in pain and relaxed his hold on her enough to allow Marigold freedom to make her next move. Twisting around towards the man, she drove her right knee up to where it would do most good, or harm depending upon which end of the knee one was at.

The man's pain-filled curses died off in a yell of sheer torment. Clutching at the point where the knee struck him, he folded over like a closing jackknife. Marigold had not finished with him. The vanity bag still swung from her arm, but she slid it free, gripped the top in both hands, pivoted and brought it around, then up like a baseball batter driving for a home run. Mark heard the solid, far too solid, thud of the bag's collision with the man's face. The hardcase spun around and piled up over the legs of the man Mark had thrown against the wall.

Light flooded into the alley as the saloon's door flew

open. The floor manager and a couple of burly bouncers
burst out, skidding to a stop and staring at the sight before
them.

"What the—!" began the manager.

Marigold leaned against the saloon's wall, her hat awry
and her shawl lying at her feet. Bending, she took up the
shawl, then waved a hand to the groaning quartet.

"It's all right, Mr. Cahill," she said. "These—er—gentlemen—must have been drinking and became a little too
impulsive."

"Do you want for me to send for Joel Stocker and have
'em jailed?"

"No. I don't think that will be necessary. They've
learned their lesson. Take them around the back, douse
them with water and send them on their way."

"Sure," the manager agreed, nodding to the bouncers.
"Do you want one of the boys to walk you to the hotel?"

"I'm going that way myself," Mark said, stepping forward. "May I have the honor of escorting you, ma'am?"

"Why thank you, sir," she replied, dropping a graceful
curtsy. "I gratefully accept your kind offer."

After setting her hat right, Marigold offered Mark her
arm and they walked together to the hotel. On learning his
name, Marigold gave Mark a long, appraising glance, then
suggested they have supper together.

After the meal Mark and Marigold went upstairs to the
bedroom floor. Mark's room lay to the left of the stairs, but
Marigold made no attempt to loosen her hold on his arm
and steered him to the right.

"I don't suppose you'd care to come to my room for a few
moments, would you, Mr. Counter?" Marigold asked, then
her hand fluttered to her lips and she dropped her gaze to
the floor. "My, doesn't that sound forward of me? I realize I
should never invite you unchaperoned to my room—but
you *are* a *Southern* gentleman, aren't you?"

"Why sure, ma'am," Mark replied. "Darned if I'm not."

Marigold took a key from her vanity bag and passed it to
Mark. Unlocking the door, he followed her into the room,
crossing to the table and turning up the lamp's wick to give
better light. The room looked much like Mark's across the

hall, except that it had three chairs at the table and a sidepiece as well as a closet.

A click came to Mark's ears. Turning, he saw Marigold had closed the door and twisted the key in the lock. Feeling his eyes on her, Marigold swung towards him. The demure expression and wide-eyed innocence stayed on her face, but not in her eyes.

"It blows open unless I keep it locked," she said, coming towards the table. "Now, what can I do to entertain you?"

Mark had a few ideas, but kept them to himself. Although puzzled at Marigold's actions, he decided to go along with her for a time. It could be the old badger game —where an irate "husband" or "fiancé" dashed in to demand money or satisfaction for the alienation of his woman's affections—but Mark doubted if Marigold would be involved in such a game. Or if she was involved, Mark gave her credit for being too intelligent to believe he would make a profitable victim.

Crossing to the window, Marigold looked out, then she drew the curtains and turned to walk to the sidepiece. After rummaging in the top drawer, Marigold took out a deck of cards. Mark had been watching her and something told him she had picked the deck out of several in the drawer.

"I know," she said, crossing the room towards where he sat at the table and tossing her vanity bag onto the bed. "Teach me to play poker."

"Here it comes!" Mark thought.

Without removing either hat or shawl, Marigold sat facing him across the table. She opened the card box, tipped out the cards, shoved the jokers back into the box and tossed it aside. Without offering the deck to be shuffled or cut, she began to deal. This puzzled Mark for he knew he had enough card savvy not to forget two such basic, but important, details. However, he kept his mouth shut and waited to see what would happen next.

Five cards landed on the table before him and Marigold set down the remainder of the deck in the center of the table. Mark took up his cards, watching her pick her own hand up. Fanning out his cards between his fingers, Mark blinked at what he saw. Ace, king, queen, jack, ten—all hearts.

Studying the cards, Mark felt even more puzzled. Three obvious conclusions leapt to mind: first, she had made a mistake and dealt him the hand from the cold deck intended for herself; second, that the deal was fair enough and the straight flush came out, as it might be expected to do once in 649,740 hands; third, she deliberately dealt him the hand for some purpose of her own, although he could not imagine what the purpose might be.

Whatever the answer, Mark held an unbeatable hand as the jokers, which were sometimes played as wild cards— and made it possible to have four of a kind and a joker which beat a straight flush—were in the box and out of the game.

"What stakes?" he asked, watching her face, but failing to read anything on it.

Marigold looked horrified at the suggestion.

"Land-sakes a-mercy!" she gasped. "You surely don't think a lady would play cards for money with a gentleman —alone in her room?"

"I apologize, ma'am."

"I think you could call me Marigold, if I may be permitted to address you as Mark."

"Reckon we have known each other long enough for that," Mark agreed. "What now, Marigold?"

Studying her cards for a moment, Marigold removed her hat and dropped it on the third chair.

"Just for fun, I'll open with my hat," she said and lifted her eyes to his face, an open challenge in them. "It's not like playing for money—now is it?"

"Nope," remarked Mark, taking his Stetson from where it hung on the back of the chair. "I'll see the hat, and raise you my bandana."

"Are we playing table stakes?" she asked, looking coyly at him.

"It's the only way. Your bet."

"Hum! My shawl to cover the bandana."

Lifting her right leg onto the chair which held the stakes, Marigold drew up her skirt. The leg was strong, had shape to it under the black stockings. Mark was willing to concede that it was as good a leg as he had seen—well, since early that morning. Marigold unclipped suspender fasteners and slid the stocking down, removed it and the shoes, then repeated the process with her left leg.

"My shoes and stockings to raise," she went on. "A gentleman would have looked the other way."

"I was always taught never to look away from the table when playing poker," Mark replied, hooking off his boots. "I'll see that bet and raise."

The raising and re-raising went on for a few more rounds and at last Marigold stared wide-eyed at the chair which held the stakes.

"Why I do declare! I just haven't another thing to raise with. Unless I can go to the closet and—"

"Huh huh! When you play table stakes, you just play for what you bring to the table with you. That's the rules, according to Hoyle."

"Is it though? But if neither of us have anything with which to bet, what do we do?"

Mark grinned. "Turn the cards and have us a showdown."

Flipping over his cards, Mark exposed them before the girl's gaze. She stared down at them with complete innocence in her expression.

"Heavens to Betsy," she said, turning over her own cards, "you have just the same hand as I have."

"Sure looks that way," he agreed and reached out to turn the lamp's wick down so its flame guttered away and was gone.

"You know, Mark," Marigold said, her chair scraping back. "There are actually men who would take advantage of an unprotected, defenseless girl at a time like this."

"The dirty dogs," he replied. "No Southern gentleman would do such a thing."

He sensed rather than saw her, felt her hand close on his, pulling at it gently but insistently.

The night outside was dark and still. The bright stars did not show through the curtains at the windows and the room lay pitch-black.

"What's the swelling on your neck?" Marigold's voice asked.

"Something bit me," Mark replied.

Silence for a moment, then Marigold said gently, "You mean like this?"

Laying down the razor he had collected during the night, Mark Counter washed his face. He looked in the mirror above the washstand and touched the oval-shaped lump on the left side of his neck, comparing it with its mate at the right. Luckily they were about level in height and his bandana would cover them. His honorable wounds might attract some attention, but he reckoned he stood big enough to handle it.

"Mark," Marigold said, sitting on the edge of the bed and looking as sedate and demure as ever, as she fastened the top button on her blouse. "What are we going to do today?"

Which Mark had also been wondering about. He had his business to attend to and, despite the time being almost nine o'clock, hoped to have it done by four or five in the afternoon. By that time Calamity Jane would be back in town and Mark couldn't see her taking kindly to Marigold's competition.

"I have to go out to the Gamble spread," he said.

She gave him a long, worried look, then smiled and brightened up a little.

"May I come along? We could hire a buggy and take a picnic basket with us."

"That'd be great," Mark replied. "I'll go hire a buggy from Pop Larkin right after breakfast, and you get the basket from the kitchen."

"Come on then," she said eagerly, jumping to her feet and holding out her hand. "Let's go."

"Slow down there, gal," he grinned. "Let me at least put my shirt on first. We don't want folks to think anything has been going on in here, now do we?"

On his way to the livery barn, Mark saw the town marshal ambling towards him along the sidewalk. Much to Mark's surprise, Stocker did not speak, or even appear to notice him.

"She must be some gal," Mark said.

"Huh?" Stocker grunted, halting, then he grinned sheepishly. "Sorry, Mark, I was thinking."

"Yeah, and when a feller's thinking that thoughtful, there's usually a right purty lil gal at the end of it."

"For you danged Texas rebs, maybe, but not for us serious-minded Montanans."

"That being the case, how do you come to keep on having any little Montanans?" Mark asked.

"We know there's a time and place for everything," Stocker replied. "Right now I'm thinking about a killing."

"Anybody I know?"

"You had a nodding acquaintance with him last night—or should I say a throwing-at-a-wall acquaintance with him?"

"That went right by me without me drawing bead on it."

"He was one of the four yahoos you 'n' Miss Tremayne tangled with in the alley last night," Stocker explained and, before Mark could ask the question which rose to his lips, carried on. "Why sure, I saw it all. Was just fixing to butt in and help the lady when you arrived. Saw you could take 'em and didn't want to spoil your fun."

"Why bless your good lil Yankee heart," grinned Mark, then he became serious. "Who killed him?"

"Framant."

"Fair fight?"

"Looks that way," Stocker admitted. "It happened down in the Black Cat Café where that feller was having breakfast. Framant come in and told him he wanted to see him outside. The feller got up and went for his gun, started first. Framant didn't even use his shotgun, drew his Colt and put one through the feller's head."

"I'll buy it," Mark drawled. "Who was the feller?"

"Don't know what name he was using in town. Framant had a wanted dodger on him under the name of Wicker. Stands to collect seven hundred dollars on him."

"Reckon he's the reason Framant came here?"

"Maybe," Stocker grunted, looking sleepily towards the hotel. "Had three pards with him in the Crystal Palace when I looked in last night."

"I never saw you," Mark drawled.

"You was too busy a-drinking, gambling and carousing. Saw Framant sat near to them four, but he didn't make a move."

"Like you said, there was four of them. Maybe he didn't like the odds."

"Could be," Stocker admitted. "Went around looking for Wicker's three pards, but they've left town. Feller down to the livery barn on Clark Street says they pulled out right after the shooting. Wonder what they wanted from Miss Tremayne?"

"Likely figured she'd be carrying her cut of the game and figured to relieve her of it," Mark suggested.

"Yep! Well, I got me an office to run. You fixing to ride out to Tom Gamble's place today?"

"Soon as I hire a buggy. I'm taking Marigold along and we aim to have a picnic on the way back."

Stocker studied Mark with admiration. No other man in town, and plenty had tried, even got to the stage where they could call the Crystal Palace's lady blackjack dealer by her first name.

"How'd you do it?" he asked.

"Us rebs have to stick together in the hostile North," Mark replied. "And now, sir, you-all causing me to keep a lady waiting."

"See you," grunted Stocker and ambled away whistling.

A grin flickered across Mark's face for he recognized Stocker's tune to be "Dixie."

That slow-moving, sleepy-looking marshal had a far quicker set of wits than a man would think just by looking at him. Mark knew Stocker had something on his mind. Something to do with the shooting that morning. Maybe Stocker was wondering, as Mark wondered, why a man holding a shotgun, and in the right, should take time out to draw a revolver.

On his return with the buggy, Mark found Marigold standing in front of the hotel. A picnic basket covered by a clean checkered cloth lay on the sidewalk at her feet. In her right hand she held her vanity bag, but in her left—

"I thought you might like this along," Marigold said, tossing his Winchester to him. "Don't look so surprised. I asked the hall clerk for your key, told him you had forgotten something. The closet seemed the most likely place for you to have left your rifle."

"And I've got the key in my pocket," he pointed out.

"Yes," she replied in a tone which hinted the subject was closed.

Jumping down, Mark helped Marigold into the buggy, went to the other side and swung in beside her.

"I'll take the reins, if you wish," she said.

This had long been the accepted Western convention. The woman handled the team and left the man free to use his weapons in an emergency. Marigold appeared to be fully capable of handling the spirited horse Pop Larkin had guaranteed to be the best buggy-hauling critter in Montana and one which would eat the trip to Tom Gamble's ranch.

For the first couple of miles Mark and Marigold talked of this and that, and the girl showed a surprisingly wide range of knowledge. She clearly had done a good bit of traveling around the West. Somehow or other the conversation turned to the holdup in Newton.

"Way I heard it," Mark said, "those fellers hadn't much of an idea how to handle the job. They hit the bank at evening, when there was only one teller in it. Then they only took thirty thousand, although there was nearly three times that in the vault."

"Maybe they didn't have time to get more," Marigold replied.

"That's what the teller said. Allows their lookout yelled that somebody was coming and they took off like the devil after a yearling. Only when he got outside there wasn't anybody in sight and he had to go and yell for help."

"That sounds like the gang spooked, or bad management."

"I bet you could have handled it better."

Just why he said it, Mark would never know. It may have been a clumsily worded compliment, meant to show his appreciation of her ability. Or it could have been a blind flash of intuition. Certainly he meant little enough by the words.

A low hiss left Marigold's lips. Her right hand dipped into the vanity bag, came out again with something in it. Mark felt that something boring into his side.

"How long have you known?" she asked, her voice sounding as it did when she saw the girl steal Mark's wallet.

"Known what?" Mark replied, looking down.

"That I'm Belle Starr."

For a long moment Mark did not reply. He looked down at the gun boring into his side. At first glance it looked like a Navy Colt. Marigold—or Belle Starr—held it like she knew which end the bullet left from. She held the hammer back under her thumb and her forefinger curled around the trigger.

"I didn't know," he said. "But come to think of it, that explains a couple of things which have been bothering me since we met."

"Such as?"

"Like why the four hardcases were watching you last night. Why you didn't scream for help when they jumped you in the alley. If you had, and they'd been caught, they might have told Joel Stocker who you are. And like why you wanted me around last night, so they couldn't slip in on you while you slept."

"That wasn't the only reason, Mark," she answered. "But it was one of them and I don't think you've cause to complain."

"I'm not complaining. What're they after? Do they reckon you know where the money from the Newton bank job is?"

"*They* reckon I know," she agreed.

"And do you?" Mark asked innocently.

The gun bored a little harder.

"I do not!" she snorted. "Land-sakes, Mark, do you think I'd be working with a fool bunch of green hands like that lot must have been? I wasn't even near Newton when the hit happened."

"Where were you?"

"On the way here from my folks' place down in the Indian Nations."

"Why here?" he went on.

"Elkhorn's growing," she replied. "The banker here is a fat, bulging-eyed pillar of the church with more money than it's decent for anybody but a Southern gentleman to have. So I figure to relieve him of some of it—but not with a gun. His kind fall easy, get them in the right conditions.

Only he's gone east on vacation and so I'm getting things set up ready."

"You've done it real well," he smiled. "Maybe just a little mite overdone, but just right for the audience. Put the gun away."

"Why?"

"You aren't going to use it, Marigold—or can I call you Belle?"

"Feel free, if you're so sure I won't use the gun."

"You won't use it for two reasons. One, you know I wouldn't turn you in."

"And the other?" she asked, not moving the gun, but keeping the buggy rolling across the range.

"Those three yahoos from last night are following us."

"Soskin's bunch?" she breathed and looked back.

Mark's left hand stabbed down, closing over the cylinder of her revolver. He dropped his thumb so it lay between the hammer and the percussion cap. The move was done only just in time. On feeling her revolver grabbed, Belle's finger closed on the trigger and she released the hammer. Instead of it striking the percussion cap and firing the chamber's contents, the hammer landed harmlessly on Mark's thumbnail.

A sudden twist plucked the gun from Belle's hand. She clenched her fists and glared at Mark, then dropped her eyes to the gun.

"Oh, Mark!" she gasped, reaching out to draw the hammer back to the half-cock position. "I'm sorry."

"My fault," he replied, changing his hold and placing the hammer down after turning the cylinder so the striker rested between two of the percussion caps.

For the first time Mark saw the revolver was not a Navy Colt. It appeared to be one of the copies produced by various little companies during the Civil War, when the relaxing of patent restrictions gave them a chance to sneak in and grab a quick profit. The gun looked better made than many of the copies and its cylinder had only five chambers, instead of the Navy Colt's six.

"A Manhattan, isn't it?" he asked, offering the weapon butt forward to the girl.

"Yes. I like its balance," she replied. "Are Soskin and his bunch on our trail, or were you only bluffing?"

"Take a peek and see."

She obeyed, and saw.

"They're following."

"Would a Southern gentleman lie to a lady?" Mark grinned. "Who are they?"

"Two-bit long riders," she answered. "Must have seen me down in the Nations some time and recognized me. Soskin, he's the one who jumped you first, he runs the bunch. Wicker was the one you splattered against the wall. Varney's the one I used my knee on. And Carter—hey, there are only three of them after us."

"Framant killed Wicker this morning."

A shudder ran through Belle's frame and she moved closer to Mark at the mention of the bounty hunter's name. Ordinary men did not scare Belle Starr, but she knew Framant would kill her without thinking twice about it; shoot her in the back, if he thought he could get away with it, rather than take a chance.

"Does he know who you are?"

"No. That wanted poster in the saloon is flattering, but nothing like me," she replied. "What about those three?"

"What about them?" Mark countered.

"Mark," she said quietly. "I had nothing to do with that holdup in Newton. I give *you* my word on that."

"And I believe you, gal," he replied, bending to take up the rifle. "Let's show them we know they're there. Stop the buggy."

Without argument, she obeyed, nursing the Manhattan on her lap as she brought the buggy to a halt. Mark stood up in the buggy and turned to face the men. His action caused them to bring their horses to a halt and show some consternation at finding their presence discovered. Taking off his hat with his left hand, holding the rifle in his right, Mark gave the men a wave 'round.

In the sign language of the range country, to take off the hat and wave it from left to right around the head when looking at approaching riders meant keep away, you are not wanted. If the warning should be ignored, the next move came from Mark's rifle in the shape of a flat-nosed .44 bullet powered by twenty-eight grains of powder.

The three men clearly understood the sign. One of them reached down towards the butt of his rifle.

"Get set, gal!" Mark warned.

"I'm set," she replied calmly. "Anyways, they won't make a fight of it."

If Belle did not know the men, she judged their characters correctly. Before the man reached his rifle, one of the others stopped him. They sat their horses for a moment, pointing and talking, then turned and rode away.

"You called the play right," Mark drawled, not relaxing his hold of the rifle's foregrip and small of the butt; he had put his hat on his head after giving the wave 'round, so as to be ready for action.

"Sure. I know their kind. Especially that bunch. Cheap, nasty and not brave. They saw me at my folks' place and know how far they can push me. And they'll reckon that wherever you are Captain Fog and the Ysabel Kid won't be far away. So I don't reckon they'll fix to tangle with us."

Mark guessed he could take Belle's summing up of the situation as being accurate. She had been raised in the Indian Nations, Oklahoma Territory, a haunt of badly wanted outlaws of all kinds. Growing up among such men, Belle had learned to know them. Some were lions, afraid of nothing, honest within their code and lights. Others, like the trio following them, were coyotes, sneaky, treacherous, deadly if they had the other side at a disadvantage. Thinking that Mark's very able friends Dusty Fog and the Ysabel Kid might be around, those three would not risk an attack which might end in Mark's death.

This belief that where Mark Counter was, his two *amigos* were sure to be, saved Mark and Belle from trouble, just as in a future meeting it would again save their lives.*

"Told you so," Belle remarked calmly.

"You told me," Mark agreed. "Let's get on our way."

She looked at him, her face troubled.

"Are you sure you still want me to go with you?"

---

* Told in *The Hard Riders* by J. T. Edson.

"Why not. You're still the girl I brought out with me—'sides which, you-all carrying the picnic basket."

A merry smile took the place of the troubled look. The old Marigold Tremayne tone came into her voice once more.

"Shall we go, sir?"

"It'd be my pleasure, ma'am," Mark replied, taking his seat and putting down the rifle.

"Then we will."

While watching Belle put the Manhattan into her vanity bag, a thought struck Mark.

"Say, weren't you scared of busting your gun when you hit that feller with your bag last night?"

"Nope," she replied and held out the bag. "Look."

The inside of the bag, apart from a few inches at the top which could be drawn together and fastened, was lined with leather. More, a holster had been built into the bag so she would always find her Manhattan's butt pointing towards the bag's mouth and protected against getting the other items in the bag entangled with its mechanism.

"I wondered why that bag didn't show the gun," he said admiringly. "That's a neat bit of work."

"My pappy made it. Let's go."

Although Mark kept a watch on their back trail, he saw no sign of the three men following. It seemed that they had either given up the chase, or waited for a chance to hit at the buggy on their return to town.

Mark collected the money from Gamble. The rancher and his wife insisted he and Belle stay for lunch and Mark had been amused at how thoroughly Marigold Tremayne replaced Belle Starr in the presence of the Gambles. She charmed Mrs. Gamble, even though the rancher's wife did not look the kind of woman to treat a saloon worker as a friend, or have the cowhands of the ranch hanging around to try to win a smile from her.

Not until they were on their return trip was any mention of the previous night's episode made.

Mark reached up a hand to adjust his bandana and Belle glanced at him, a merry twinkle in her eyes.

"Who bit you?" she asked.

"You did," Mark grinned.

"I mean first."

"Calamity Jane."

A smile flickered across Belle's lips as she studied his face, then died off again and a frown creased her brow.

"You're funning me," she said, then shook her head. "No, you're not. *Did* Calamity Jane do that to you?"

"Why sure. She's quite a gal," Mark answered. "Came through yesterday and she'll likely be back tonight."

"Will she?" Belle sniffed.

There Belle let the matter drop. Her attitude showed that she did not intend to discuss the matter of Calamity Jane further. Yet Mark's instincts warned him he had better try to keep Calamity Jane and Belle Starr well separated that night.

Belle continued to talk about various things and drive the buggy. Both she and Mark kept alert for signs of the three men, but saw none. Either the trio had decided to call the game off when they saw Belle's escort, or they were lying low and waiting until conditions favored them. Whatever the reason, Belle and Mark saw no sign of the men and reached Elkhorn without any incident.

In town Mark saw something. Calamity Jane's wagon stood behind Larkin's livery barn and her team horses in Larkin's corral. Hoping he would not come across Calamity in the street and while escorting Belle, Mark headed for the hotel.

"I'll expect to see you tonight," Belle told Mark as they stood in the passage of the hotel's upper floor. "You can bring a friend, if you like."

Reading the challenge in Belle's voice, Mark groaned silently. From the way Belle looked, and what he had seen of Calamity Jane, Mark guessed one thing. If they got together, it wouldn't be bulls locking horns that Marshal Joel Stocker had to worry about.

"I'll see you," he promised.

"Make sure you do," Belle purred. "I'd hate to have to come looking for you-all, Mark honey."

Kissing him lightly on the cheek, Belle turned and walked towards her room. Mark watched her go and grinned as he went along the passage to his. Maybe Calamity would not find him. She might even have found herself another feller by this time.

Just as he unlocked the door, Mark heard a faint scuffling noise in his room. Almost without thinking about it, his right hand dipped and lifted his Colt from leather. Gripping the doorknob, Mark pushed hard. The door swung inwards and thudded into something which gave a startled gasp. Mark had been right, he did have an unexpected visitor inside. Stepping into the room fast, Mark thrust the door closed behind him and lined his gun—on Calamity Jane.

The girl stood with her back to the wall, a look of amazement and fury on her face as she put a hand to her nose. However her eyes dropped to the barrel of the Colt lined on her and the anger left her face.

"Easy there, Mark!" she gasped. "I forgot what you come up here to collect."

"Huh?"

"That money. I should have known better than fool around like this when you're carrying it."

Now Mark understood. Calamity put his reaction down to his expecting trouble, or at least being prepared for trouble, while carrying the money he collected from Gamble. He did not disillusion her, figuring the later she learned about Belle Starr the better for all concerned.

Even as he holstered his Colt, Mark found Calamity close to him, her arms around his neck and her mouth crushing against his. She moved back a shade after the kiss, cocked her head on one side and grinned at him.

"Boy, I sure put my brand on you. Right under your right —hey! That's not on the right side! Mark Counter, what've you been doing?"

"Would you believe me if I told you I cut myself shaving?"

"Nope," she snorted.

"Now what do you reckon I've been doing, Calam?" he went on.

"I just wouldn't want to guess."

There did not seem to be any point in standing talking. So Mark did the next best thing. He scooped Calamity into his arms and kissed her. While it had nothing to do with the subject under discussion, it sure ended Calamity's curiosity faster than a whole heap of lip-flapping would have.

"Let's paint the town tonight, Mark," Calamity suggested when he released her, and went on innocently, "that's a swell-looking saloon next door."

"There's a couple of other nice places—"

"Sure," Calamity interrupted, "but they don't have blackjack games."

"Blackjack?" Mark asked, sounding nonchalant and innocent.

"Blackjack!" Calamity repeated. "They do tell me the dealer totes a real mean picnic basket."

Standing back from Mark, Calamity put her hands on her hips and grinned, her even white teeth flashing. He grinned back. There was something infectious about Calamity Jane's zest for living. Maybe she did not conform to the rigid conventions imposed on women of her day, but she enjoyed every minute of her life.

Then Mark remembered how Belle Starr smiled when she invited him to bring Calamity to the saloon that night. They were two of a kind, those girls. A man couldn't judge them by the same moral standards which affected other women. Each girl lived her life the way she felt it ought to be lived, and stuck to certain rigid codes. The main difference between Belle and Calamity was in the way their lives had gone. Calamity stayed on the right side of the law, Belle strayed over its line and went against it.

"How'd you get to know?" Mark asked.

"You know how folks talk," Calamity grinned.

"Old Pop Larkin!" Mark snorted. "Darned old goat, never knew a livery barn owner who wouldn't talk the hindleg off a hoss. How did you get in here?"

"Bet my door key'll open every room on the floor," Calamity answered. "Did she do that?"

"She's a Southern lady," Mark replied, spreading his bandana to hide his honorable wounds.

"Does that mean yes or no?" grinned Calamity. "Go wash up, then we'll head for the Crystal Palace and play us some blackjack."

* * *

Mark's hopes of keeping Calamity and Belle apart did not seem very great. They sank to zero as he and Calamity prepared to go down to the hotel dining room and have a meal before visiting the Crystal Palace.

Even as he stepped into the passage with Calamity at his side, Mark saw the door to Belle's room open. It appeared that Belle had been waiting for his appearance, for she walked towards him. They met at the head of the stairs and Belle directed a dazzling smile at Calamity.

"Why, Mark," she said, in her Marigold voice, "you-all never said the Ysabel Kid was in town."

While the light in the passage was poor, it was not *that* poor. Mark knew it; Belle knew it; and, if the way Mark felt the girl's body stiffen and bristle at his side was any indication, Calamity knew it too.

"Miss Tremayne," Mark said, for he had not let on to Calamity the secret of Belle's true identity. "Allow me to present Miss Martha Jane Canary. Miss Canary, this is Miss Marigold Tremayne."

Belle showed well-simulated shock and embarrassment at her "mistake." Her hand fluttered to her mouth and her eye took on an expression of horror as she looked Calamity up and down.

"Land-sakes!" Belle gasped. "How *could* I have made such a mistake? Why I hear the Ysabel Kid is good looking."

Hearing the sudden intake of breath at his side, Mark prepared to grab Calamity before she jumped Belle. He did not know Calamity very well. The girl might lack some formal education, but she had a quick set of wits sharpened by her contacts with men and women of all kinds.

"That's real swell blond hair you have, honey," she replied. "Why do you dye the roots black?"

"Perhaps you'd like to try to see if they are black?" Belle replied.

"Any time. Right—right nice of you to invite me and Mark to join you for supper, Miss Tremayne. We'll accept."

The change in Calamity's speech came due to a man and woman emerging from one of the rooms. Before either girl could say another word, Mark gripped them by an arm each and hustled them down the stairs.

Mark enjoyed his supper. His worries that the girls might start a brawl in the dining room died away. Neither Calamity nor Belle cared greatly for public opinion, but they did know any brawl started in the hotel would be ended quickly. So they contented themselves in firing barbed, biting, catty comments at each other. On the face of it, honors appeared about equal when Mark took their arms and walked them to the saloon.

Interested eyes watched them enter the saloon and cross to the bar. None of the people in the saloon failed to notice that Belle—or as they thought of her, Marigold Tremayne—did not follow her usual procedure of going upstairs to remove her hat. Also they all knew that Marigold Tremayne never accepted drinks, or went near the bar. An eagerly expectant air ran through the room, following the whispered information that the other gal was Calamity Jane.

"What'll it be, ladies?" Mark asked, resigned to the fact that there would be a clash and that he could not stop it.

"Whisky for me," Calamity replied.

"I'll have a brandy, Mark," Belle went on.

"*Brandy?*" Calamity gasped. "French hawgwash!"

"A *lady* doesn't drink whisky," Belle replied, and getting no reaction to her emphasis of the word lady, tried another attack. "It's fattening. Of course, darling, with a figure like yours, what have you to lose?"

"You're so right," Calamity purred back. "At my age you can eat and drink what you like. But not when you get as old as you are."

Once more Calamity had come back with a cat-clawing answer that evened the score with Belle. Angrily Belle's fingers drummed on the bar top while she sought for a suitable comment. Calamity grinned at her, enjoying the duel of words and not wanting it to end for a spell.

Twisting her whisky glass between her fingers, Calamity turned her back to the bar and leaned her elbows on its mahogany top. She looked around the room and her eyes came to rest on the board with the wanted posters. Crossing the room, Calamity came to a halt and studied the center poster, cocking her head to one side and looking at the addition to the official wording.

"The toughest gal in the West!" she read in explosive, snorting words. "Now that's not right at all."

Watched by everybody in the room, Calamity dug a stump of pencil from her pants pocket. She leaned a hand on the small table somebody had placed before the board and reached out to write "2nd" between the first two words of the message.

"That's better," she said.

At the bar Belle clenched her hands into fists and started to move. Mark's hand caught her arm and held her.

"Easy, Belle," he whispered. "Calam doesn't know who you are. At least, I haven't told her. And Framant's sat over there watching."

For a moment Mark thought Belle would show enough sense to at least wait until Calamity came back to the bar, then find some other excuse to start a fight. Maybe she would have, for Belle had put time and money into setting herself up in Elkhorn ready to pluck dollar-sign-marked feathers from the local banker's tail, except for Calamity's next action.

"Let's just pretty old Belle up a mite while I'm at it," Calamity went on and began to pencil in a mustache on the picture's top lip.

Calamity did not notice Belle had crossed the room to her side. Mark knew she had, for his shin hurt where she kicked him and caused him to release her arm. With a shrug, he leaned on the bar. Things had gone too far now, he could not stop the inevitable.

All eyes went to the table, watching Belle reach out and take the pencil from Calamity's fingers. Everybody, with the exception of Mark, wondered what their lady blackjack dealer meant to do and why.

Placing her hip against Calamity's, Belle thrust hard and sent the redhead staggering a few paces. Then, as Calamity caught her balance and stopped, Belle put down her vanity bag and leaned over to score out Calamity's addition to the poster.

"I've never met the lady," Belle remarked, ignoring the interest her action aroused among the people in the room. "But I'm sure the statement was correct."

At his table, Framant leaned forward, studying Belle with cold eyes.

Unbuckling her gunbelt, Calamity put it down on the table by Belle's bag. She dipped her shoulder and charged Belle, sending her sprawling. Belle caught the wall and prevented herself falling, but her hat slid back and she brushed it from her head. By this time Calamity had picked up the pencil which Belle dropped and turned to the poster once more.

Belle sprang forward and Calamity twisted to face her, sitting on the table and raising her feet ready to thrust the blonde away. Only Belle did not come in range. Shooting out her hands, she grabbed for Calamity's ankles and caught hold of the cuffs of her pants instead. Calamity let out a yell of anger and surprise as Belle threw her weight back and heaved. Although she tried to grab something, Calamity failed to find anything she might grip to prevent herself being dragged from the table. She landed on the floor with a thud, but Belle had not finished. Backing away, Belle dragged Calamity across the floor, the other girl bending her legs and thrusting, trying to force herself free and grabbing at chairs or table legs to avoid being hauled along.

To the tune of laughter and shouts of encouragement, Belle dragged Calamity across the floor. There was only one way out for Calamity, although not a way a more modest young woman would have cared to take. Unbuckling her waist belt, she tried to slide out of her pants. Their tightness held her and she grabbed the leg of the faro table as she passed it. This proved firm enough, and the table heavy enough, to anchor her down. Belle grunted and threw her weight back to try to tear Calamity free. Too late she realized what Calamity had done. The pants started to slide and Calamity gave a heave which freed herself. She left her pants in Belle's hands and lost her moccasins.

Taken by surprise, Belle staggered back, lost her footing, and sat down hard, still clinging to Calamity's pants. Calamity, still wearing her kepi, made a pretty picture, her shirttail flapping around her shapely bare legs and giving glimpses of the new white, lace-frilled combination chemise and drawers she had bought that afternoon to prove to Mark Counter that she was a real lady at heart. They were the latest fashion among show people, short legged and daring, and Calamity had the sort of figure to set them off to their best advantage.

Coming to her feet, Calamity flung herself at Belle, landing on the blonde before she was on her feet. Grabbing down, Calamity gripped Belle's skirt and heaved at it with all her strength. Belle gave a yell, tried to twist herself free and in doing so threw the final pressure on the tortured cloth. With a ripping sound, the skirt tore from waist almost to hem. Rearing back, her trophy firmly gripped in both hands, Calamity tore the skirt away, rolling Belle right over and leaving her black stocking-clad legs, with frilly red garters, and black drawers as brief and attractive as Calamity's own, exposed by the hem of her blouse.

Once more Calamity sprang into the attack, her hands closing on Belle's blouse. Belle forced herself up, her own hands gripped Calamity's shirt neck and her eyes met Calamity's.

"Try it!" Belle spat out. "And I'll peel you raw."

For once in her life Calamity Jane backed down from a challenge. Nothing she had seen about the blonde told her Belle would not carry out the threat of stripping Calamity naked, even if it meant losing every stitch of clothing she wore in the process. Modesty did not prevent Calamity from calling Belle's bluff. She knew that if they did start to remove more clothing, the owners of the saloon would stop the fight. A hair-yanking brawl between two women was common enough for the owners to let one go on; it was regarded as being a bit of added entertainment for the customers. But there were limits to how far the owners dare let such a fight go.

So Calamity released her hold of Belle's blouse, for she did not want what promised to be a good fight stopped. Not until she had handed that blond hussy the licking of her life as a warning to stay away from Calamity Jane's man.

While releasing Belle's blouse, Calamity made up her mind how to handle the situation. She had been taught to fight by soldiers and freighters, men who showed her the value of a fist over hair-yanking. In more than one saloon brawl this knowledge had given her a decided edge over the other girl.

"First one into her belly," Calamity thought. "Then the next to her jaw."

The first drove into the stomach. Up came the other hand and caught the down-dropping jaw—

And Calamity hit the floor on her rump, her head spinning. She had learned an important lesson. The other girl also knew how to use her fists.

Now it was Belle's turn to become overconfident. She sprang forward and drew back her foot. Calamity showed that she had learned other lessons in the art of self-defense. Quickly she hooked her left foot behind Belle's left ankle, placed her right foot on Belle's left knee, pulled on the ankle and pushed on the knee. Caught with her other leg raised for the kick, Belle could not stop herself going over, but she broke the worst of her fall with her hands.

They came up and flung themselves at each other. For a time it might have been two men fighting. They used their fists, wrestling throws and holds, none of the usual tactics of a pair of fighting women. The watching crowd yelled their encouragement and already the house gamblers were taking bets on the results. Not that they had any clear indication of which girl would win for they seemed evenly matched.

"Howdy, Mark," a sleepy voice said.

Turning from watching Belle drive Calamity back into the crowd with a battery of punches, Mark looked at the speaker.

"Howdy, Joel. What're you fixing to do about this? Speaking as a duly appointed officer of the law that is."

"Ain't doing nothing," Stocker replied, watching the crowd scatter as the two girls spun around and through them. "My job's to keep the peace and I wouldn't reckon anybody's breaking it." He paused and eyed Mark with that same sleepy gaze. "How do you figure in on this?"

"Could say I brought them together," Mark admitted. "But, knowing Calamity, she'd've come in here and tangled with somebody, and B—Marigold's the most likely one for her to pick from."

"Huh huh!" Stocker grunted. "Figured it that way my-

self. Only I wouldn't have expected Miss Marigold to be the
one. Allus struck me as being a real lady."

The "real lady" was at that moment swinging Calamity
around by the hair and sent her sprawling across the room
to hit the wall. Calamity seemed dazed by the impact and
stood with legs apart, back braced against the wall.

"Best stop—!" Stocker began as Belle moved in towards
Calamity.

His words stopped, for Belle did not deliver a crippling
kick at her helpless opponent. Instead she stopped and
started to slap Calamity's face, alternating hands and
swinging the other girl's head from side to side. The pain of
the slaps revived Calamity and she thrust forward, her
hands tangling into Belle's hair. If Belle's yell of pain was
anything to go by, the grip Calamity had on her hurt.

The fight developed into a more female brawl with
Calamity's hair-yanking opening. Reeling backwards, the
two girls spun across the room in a flailing tangle of arms
and legs, pulling hair, swinging slaps and punches. One
piece of feminine fighting was denied them. Calamity's
work did not tend to allow her to grow long nails, and Belle
knew men objected to playing with a gambler who had
long enough fingernails to make identifying nicks on the
cards.

Even without scratching, the two girls put on a tolerable
example of the art of barroom brawling. On their feet, or
rolling over and over on the floor, they went at it for almost
fifteen minutes without a pause.

Then Belle was flat on her back and Calamity dropped to
kneel astride her with the intention of grabbing her hair
and bouncing her head on the floor. Belle knew as well as
Calamity what the redhead intended to do. Bringing up
her legs, Belle hooked them under Calamity's armpits
from behind, almost as if she was trying to perform a full
nelson with legs instead of arms. Calamity gave a yell as she
went over backwards, but kept on rolling to land on her
feet and then dropped down. She landed on Belle's raised
feet, felt them against her chest and knew what to expect
even if she could not prevent it happening.

Thrusting up with her feet, Belle sent Calamity flying
backwards across the room to land on a tabletop. Calamity

saw Belle coming at her and rolled back off the table, throwing it over. It landed on Belle's right foot, the edge thudding down on her toes. Belle squealed in pain. She was still hopping on her other foot when Calamity rounded the table.

Calamity swung herself around, her fist coming in a circle which ended on the side of Belle's jaw. The crowd scattered as Belle went sprawling across the room, hit the bar and clung to it. Dazedly Belle watched Calamity come forward, a chair gripped in her hands ready to strike. The blonde sobbed for breath, she tried to force herself from the bar to avoid the blow.

"We'd better stop Calam," Mark said to Stocker.

"Ye—dagnabit, look there."

Instead of lifting the chair and crashing it onto Belle, Calamity threw it to one side. She staggered to the bar and Belle crouched ready to fight back.

"H—hold it!" Calamity gasped.

"H—had e—enough?" Belle replied in surprise.

"No—no—Feel like a drink."

"A—and me. Fred, whisky and brandy."

"What do you make of that?" Stocker asked.

"Those gals sure must be enjoying the fight. Belle could have finished Calamity against the wall there, and Calamity could sure have sung B—Marigold to sleep with that chair. There's been other times when they could have used a knee or foot and didn't."

He hoped Stocker had not noticed the slip he made in his words. Not by a flicker of emotion did Stocker's sleepy face show he had noticed Mark say "Belle" instead of Marigold. However, Mark would have been surprised if he had seen anything on the marshal's face even if he noticed the slip.

The girls finished their drinks. Watching them, the crowd grew expectant once more. Most of the onlookers had felt disappointed when they saw the fight come to such an indecisive end. Now they realized that the fight had not ended, but that the opponents were just taking a drink while regaining their strength for a resumption of hostilities.

From his place at the end of the bar, Mark watched the girls and felt puzzled. While he could understand Calamity grandstanding in such a manner, it surprised him that Belle would act in the same way.

"My turn," Calamity said, slapping her empty glass on the counter. "Same again, Fred."

"Here's looking at you," Belle replied, raising her glass. "Not that you'd be seeing much with that eye."

"If it's worse than yours, it's bad," Calamity grinned. "Whooee, that was a mean one you caught me with at the beginning. Say, where'd you learn to wrestle?"

"From an Indian. Have you finished?"

"Sure."

Setting down her glass, Calamity lashed out her fist, driving it into the blonde's jaw and spinning her in a circle to hit the bar. Belle swung her arm sideways, the heel of her hand driving into Calamity's ribs and stopping her forward rush.

For thirty minutes by the barroom clock the fight raged, from start to when the two girls, tottering on legs which looked like heat-buckled candles, gave Stocker cause to think he might have to end the fight.

"I'll have to stop 'em if they go any further, Mark," the marshal said as Calamity staggered from a push and left her torn shirt in Belle's hands.

"Looks that way," Mark replied, for Belle had lost her blouse.

It could not go on. The girls were on their last reserves of strength. Where their slaps had sounded like whip cracks on landing, they now barely made a sound and on reaching flesh seemed more in the nature of a gentle push.

Hooking a leg behind Calamity, more by accident than design, Belle tripped her. They were locked in each other's arms and could do nothing to stop themselves falling. However, Calamity managed to twist herself so they both hit the floor. Their arms relaxed and they rolled apart, lying flat on their backs, breasts heaving, mouths hanging open.

"Get the doctor," Mark said. "I'll get the gals to their rooms."

"Sure," Stocker replied, "I'll—man, just look at that."

Incredibly, in view of the grueling brawl they had just fought, Belle was trying to sit up. Beside her, Calamity rolled over and forced her hands against the floor. Belle did not look the elegant creature who dealt blackjack. Her once immaculate hair now resembled a tangled, dirty, blond wool mop. The face was streaked with sweat and dirt, its left eye blackened and puffed almost shut, the nose bloody. Her most serious injury was a bite on the left hand, gained when the fight was at its height. She had lost one stocking but the garter remained, a slash of color against the white of her leg. The other stocking had little foot, no knee and hung in tatters. Calamity was just as badly bruised and battered, dirty and exhausted.

Sensing a climax approaching, the crowd fell silent. Quite a lot of money depended on the outcome of the fight.

Through the whirling mist that seemed to surround her, Calamity saw Belle sitting up. Drawing on her last ounce of strength, Calamity thrust herself forward, shooting her fist at Belle. Everything went black for Calamity the instant before her fist landed. Carried by the impetus of her body, the fist caught Belle at the side of the jaw and Belle flopped onto her back. Calamity's limp form dropped onto Belle's and they lay there without a move.

"What'd you call that, Mark?" Stocker asked.

"I'd say a standoff. Go get the doc, I'll tend to the girls."

Excitement burst over the crowd, cheers and shouts of laughter ringing out. The floor manager called for drinks on the house and there was a rush to the bar. Mark did not join it. He crossed to where the saloon girls, eight in all, stood in a group, knowing they were not included in the manager's largess.

"How'd you gals like to earn five dollars each?" he asked.

"All of us?" gasped the boss girl, a big, beautiful black-haired woman, eyeing Mark with doubt and admiration.

"Not for that," Mark replied. "I want you to tote Marigold and Calamity to their rooms at the hotel."

"Sure we'll do it," grinned the boss girl. "I'm not doing anything important after that though."

"I wish I wasn't," drawled Mark and took out his wallet. "Take them in the back way."

Four girls took Calamity by the arms and legs, raising her from the floor, while the other four lifted Belle. To admiring cheers the battered girls were carried out of the saloon's rear door.

"Here, Mark," Stocker said, coming over with a couple of glasses in his big hands. "I fetched you a drink along. Being a duly appointed officer of the law, I don't get the giveaway stuff."

One sip at the contents of his glass told Mark that Stocker spoke the truth. Like most saloons, the Crystal Palace kept a stock of cheaper whisky to be used when the boss announced drinks on the house. The liquor in Mark's glass tasted like best stock. It seemed that, like Mark, the owners of the Crystal Palace were not fooled by Stocker's sleepy-acting ways and knew how to show a good lawman their appreciation.

"Man, that came from a customer's bottle," Mark said, then noticed Stocker looking around the room. "What's wrong?"

"Nothing much. I was wondering where Framant has gone."

Setting down his glass on the nearest table, Mark looked around the room. He had last seen the bounty hunter before the fight started and Framant was showing considerable interest in Belle's actions.

Without a word to Stocker about his fears, Mark turned on his heel and headed across the room towards the main doors of the saloon.

There was considerable excitement at the hotel as Mark entered its reception hall. Although the girls had carried Belle and Calamity in through the rear door, they still had to bring their groaning burdens to the front and up the stairs. In doing so, they attracted attention, their chatter bringing residents from the dining and sitting rooms to see what was happening.

Shoving through the crowd, Mark found the desk clerk, a plump, pompous young man, blocking his path.

"May I ask just what is going on, Mr. Counter?" the clerk said as Mark started up the stairs. "This is not the sort—"

His words trailed off as Mark's hands gripped him by the lapels of his coat, then lifted. The man's feet left the floor and kicked futilely as Mark set him aside. Gurgling incoherently, the clerk turned and stared after Mark as he went up the stairs. It shook a man to be picked up as if he were a baby and set aside in so casual a manner.

"Just set the blonde down, you calico cats," a voice said from the passage above. "I'll tend to her."

Three strides brought Mark to the head of the stairs and he turned the corner. It seemed he had not come a moment too soon.

"Hold it, Framant!" Mark snapped.

Standing with his shotgun in his left hand, Framant looked towards the big blond Texan. The saloon girls had laid Belle down and fallen back, flattening themselves against the walls and staring in fear at the bounty hunter.

"Keep out of this, cow nurse," Framant replied. "I'm taking her down to Newton with me."

"How long have you known who she was?" Mark replied, watching the hand which gripped the small of the shotgun's butt, its forefinger on the trigger.

"Had me suspicions since I come in," Framant growled.

"And left it until now to take her?"

"I don't take chances," Framant answered. "Now just get out of my way."

Framant bent down, reaching for Belle's arm.

"Leave her lie," Mark said quietly.

"Yeah!" the bounty hunter replied, straightening again. "Why? 'Cause you want to take her in?"

"Nope. But you hadn't the guts to stack against her while she was on her feet and you'll leave her now. Or take her through me."

A grin twisted Framant's lips as he studied the big Texan.

"That can be done easy enough."

He made a gesture to lift the shotgun in his left hand. Mark watched the move—then remembered something. Another man had faced Framant that day, and he died with a revolver bullet, not a charge of buckshot in him.

Dipping his free hand, Framant closed his fingers around the butt of his revolver and started to lift it. Just like all the others, that big Texan had been watching his shotgun, not the revolver, and would shortly pay the penalty for crossing Jubal Framant.

Too late the bounty hunter saw his mistake.

Mark's right hand dipped, the Army Colt flowed from

the holster in a liquid-smooth move. Cocking back the hammer as the gun lifted, Mark sent a bullet into Framant's head, holding his gun waist high and using instinctive alignment for he did not have time to take aim in any other way.

Shock, amazement and terror warred among themselves for expression on Framant's face an instant before Mark's bullet struck between his eyes and wiped off all expression. In that last moment Framant knew he had met a man who saw through his trick and beat him.

A girl screamed. Another turned, hiding her face in her hands. Framant's shotgun fell from his left hand, the revolver slipped from between the fingers of his right. Its barrel had barely cleared leather and it clattered to the floor, beating Framant's lifeless body by a split second.

Feet pounded on the stairs behind Mark. Stocker appeared at the head of the stairs, traveling with a speed which belied his usual lethargic pose. Holstering the big Dragoon, Stocker looked down at Belle, then towards Framant.

"What happened?"

"Framant threw down on me," Mark replied. "And I found out what he toted the shotgun for."

Turning, Stocker ordered the people who started to flock upstairs back down again. The cold tone which replaced his sleepy voice warned the crowd that they had best do as he told them without argument.

"How'd you mean, Mark," he said, after Mark had carried Belle into her room where she and Calamity now lay side by side on her bed. "You know why he toted the shotgun."

"It was a plant. Kept the other feller watching his left hand, while his right fetched out the gun. It near on caught me, only I remembered that feller he shot this morning and wondered why in hell he'd chance drawing a revolver when he held the scatter."

The local doctor arrived, having pushed his way through the crowd, showing a complete disregard for social standing as became the only medical man in almost five hundred miles.

"I'd best see about moving Framant," Stocker remarked, as the doctor went into Belle's room.

"Sure," Mark replied. "I'll go pick up the gals' belongings from the saloon. They'll not be feeling like bothering, way they're all tuckered out."

"Go ahead. You leaving town in the morning?"

"Sure," Mark agreed.

"Nothing personal, but I'll not be sorry to see you go. Be pleased to have *you* back anytime—but come alone."

Mark grinned. Having served under Dusty Fog as a deputy marshal, he could appreciate Stocker's point of view.

At the saloon, Mark gathered up Belle's vanity bag and Calamity's gunbelt. The owner of the saloon himself came over, grinning broadly.

"You sure brought our Miss Tremayne out, Mark," he said.

That the man knew his name did not surprise Mark. A saloonkeeper always tried to keep in touch with important people who used his establishment, and without false modesty Mark admitted he was well enough known to warrant such interest.

"I've got their clothes bundled up back of the bar," the man went on. "Reckon they might need them, although apart from Calamity's pants and moccasins and Miss Marigold's shoes, there's not much they'll be able to wear."

"I'll take them anyways," Mark grinned. "What they don't want I'll have built into the sugan I had made after the battle in Bearcat Annie's."*

"Was you—sure, that was while Cap'n Fog was town marshal in Quiet Town."

The battle in Bearcat Annie's saloon, where three female deputies fought it out with the saloonkeeper and her girls to allow Dusty Fog, Mark and the other male deputies a chance to enter the saloon and arrest a bunch of gunmen, had become a legend in the West. Mark had gathered the remnants of clothing and had them made into a sugan, a thick patchwork quilt, which he now carried in his bedroll.

Mark intended to have Calamity's shirt and Belle's

* Told in *Quiet Town* by J. T. Edson.

blouse and skirt added to the other material, as a memento of the occasion.

For a time Mark stayed at the saloon, talking with the owner and a number of prominent businessmen of the town. The doctor arrived with word that neither girl had sustained any really serious injury, although Belle's hand would always carry the mark of Calamity's teeth.

"Reckon I've lost my blackjack dealer for a spell," grinned the owner. "But, man, what a fight."

Soon after, Mark left the saloon, carrying the girls' belongings with him. On his way to the hotel, Mark thought of Stocker's apparent lack of interest in why Framant should be in the building. This did not fool Mark. If Stocker guessed the truth, and Mark reckoned he did, he was holding off until Belle had recovered from the brawl before seeing her.

How long Mark had been asleep, he did not know. Lying in bed in the darkness of his room, he waited for a repetition of the sound which woke him. Reaching out his right hand, he drew a Colt from where his gunbelt lay on the chair.

The door of his room inched open and he could see a shape, darker than the surrounding blackness, at it.

"Mark!" a voice whispered.

"Come ahead, Belle," he replied, swinging from the bed and reaching for his jeans.

Belle entered the room and closed the door behind her, standing still until Mark drew the curtains and lit the lamp. In its light, Mark studied Belle and a grin of admiration flickered to his lips. She wore a flimsy robe he had seen her in the previous night, but her hair and face still bore traces of the fight even though the doctor had tried to clean her up. The admiration came as a tribute to her courage, not her appearance. After that brawl, Belle could still get up and walk, if hobbling painfully.

"I'm in trouble, Mark," she said, limping to the bed and flopping down to sit on it.

"You sure look that way," he agreed.

"Framant saw me. I'm sure he knows who I am. And so does Joel Stocker."

"Don't worry about Framant," Mark said gently. "He was waiting up here for you."

Which explained itself to anybody who took a minute to think about it. The fact that Mark was still alive, and she still had her freedom, told Belle all she needed to know.

"Joel Stocker knows," Belle went on. "He's not as du—"

Her words stopped abruptly as the room door opened. Mark caught up his Colt ready to use, and Belle reached towards the second gun.

"I thought I'd find you here!" Calamity said from the doorway.

She stood for a moment, eyeing Belle with a mixture of anger and admiration. The last thing Calamity felt like doing was going visiting in her present state of health.

"Shut the door and keep your voice down, Calam," Mark snapped. "Belle's in trouble."

"I'll say she is," Calamity replied, closing the door. "B—Belle?"

"Belle Starr, the mustached lady," Belle grinned.

"You mean—you—I—you're—"

"Whatever that means, I'm still Belle Starr."

Crossing the room, Calamity flopped down beside Belle, staring at the other girl and holding the blanket draped around her shoulders.

"Belle Starr!" she said wonderingly, then held out a hand. "I'm sorry, Belle, I didn't know about it when I went to the poster. Shucks, if I had, I'd've kept away and found some other way of starting the brawl so I could hand you your things. Say, who won?"

Both girls looked at Mark expectantly, for neither could remember the details of the final stages of the fight and each felt sure she had been beaten.

"It was a standoff," he replied. "With both of you plumb tuckered out."

"That's a good way to be," Belle said and took Calamity's hand. "No hard feelings, Calam?"

"Not if you haven't. Say, was you ever in Fort Baker? There's a gal—"

"Let's leave old home week until later," Mark put in. "Belle's got troubles enough without that."

Possibly for the first time in her life Calamity looked contrite.

"Gee, I'm sorry, Belle. It's all my fa—"

"Forget it, Calam. It's as much my fault as yours. I didn't have to let you needle me right then."

"Framant won't forget it," Calamity pointed out.

"He's no worry," Belle replied. "I'm thinking about Joel Stocker. He knows I'm Belle Starr now, and Joel's too good a lawman to overlook it. He might not like doing it, but he'd take me and send me back to Newton."

Clapping a hand to her forehead, Calamity groaned. "And I'm the darned fool who caused it all. We'll just have to pull out of town tonight."

"Neither of you are in any shape to ride," Mark pointed out. "Even if Belle had a hoss."

"Which I haven't."

"You couldn't handle my blood bay, the condition you're in." Mark went on, looking at Belle. "And even if you could, the saddle's locked in Larkin's office."

"Will the marshal be coming after you tonight?" asked Calamity.

"Not if I know Joel. He'll be around in the morning when I've had time to get around to talking and walking."

"Then we've a chance," Calamity grinned. "All we need is a feller with a strong back—which we've got right here."

On hearing Calamity's plan, the other two agreed it might work. They wasted no time in preparing to put it into action.

"Calam, honey," Mark grinned, putting on his shirt. "You pair know of more ways of making me lose sleep than anybody I know."

Mark was just boosting a sick, sore and groaning Calamity onto the box of her wagon ready to leave town when Marshal Stocker strolled up. It was morning and the wagon stood ready to roll, Mark's blood-bay stallion waiting saddled for its master to mount.

"Morning, Miss Calamity, Mark," he greeted. "See you're fixing to leave."

"Why sure," Calamity grinned, settling down on the seat and reaching for the reins. "Say, have you-all seen that blond gal around? I bet she's still in bed after the whupping I handed her."

A sleepy smile twisted Stocker's lips as he looked at Calamity.

"Sure was a whupping," he grinned. "She never laid a hand on you."

"Then why'n't you stop the crowd, somebody kicked hell out of me. You tell her she'll know better'n tangle with Calamity Jane next time."

"I'd do that. Only she's up and gone."

"Gone?" Calamity gasped. "How'd you mean, gone?"

"Must've left during the night. Took her trunk and belongings and gone. Are you traveling empty, Calamity?"

"Just some of my own stuff is all."

Walking to the rear of the wagon, Stocker lifted the cover and looked inside. Apart from a fair-sized oblong object covered with a buffalo hide, the wagon contained nothing. Turning back, Stocker stepped over a pile of buffalo chips and logs lying between the wagon and the corral fence. Calamity looked back at him.

"You don't reckon I'd be hiding her in the back of my wagon after what happened last night, do you?" she asked.

"Nope, I reckon not," Stocker answered. "I'll drift along and see if I can find her around town. See you, Mark."

"Yeah, I know," Mark drawled. "You'll be around."

Throwing a warning glance at Calamity, Mark swung aboard his saddle and the blood bay walked forward. Calamity closed her mouth, took up the reins and started her wagon moving. For a few seconds Stocker stood watching them go, then he grinned, kicked the buffalo chips with his toe and slouched away.

Five minutes passed. Then three men came from a side alley where they had been watching the corral. Soskin, the leader of the trio of hardcases, walked to the corral and looked around him. Behind him, Varney and Carter stood with puzzled expressions on their faces.

"Looks like Belle's slipped out of town," Varney growled.

"How?" Carter replied. "You saw Calamity, she could hardly stand. Reckon Belle'd be in any better shape?"

"She went all right," Soskin put in, pointing down. "And that's how, only Stocker was too dumb to see it."

"What're we going to do?" asked Carter.

"Trail the wagon from well back. Then when they make camp for the night move in on them."

For three miles Mark and Calamity held an even pace, leaving the town behind them. They did not hurry, but Calamity repeatedly twisted around to look at their back trail. She noticed that Mark took no such precautions and grunted.

"What's wrong, Calam?" he asked.

"Reckon the marshal won't be following us?" she replied.

"He'll not. His jurisdiction ends on the edge of town."

"We sure put one over on him," she chuckled.

"Reckon we did, huh?"

"Don't you?"

"Nope."

They were approaching a ford over a wide though shallow river. Grinning at Mark, Calamity hauled back on the reins and slowed her team's pace.

"Shall I stop here or the other side?" she asked. "I reckon I'll go through—"

"You do and we'll take up where we left off last night!" Belle's voice yelled from under the wagon.

Laughing, Calamity brought the wagon to a halt, applied the brake and slowly climbed down from the box. Bending, she looked under the wagon to where Belle's face showed from inside the possum belly—a sweat- and dirt-streaked face, for the rawhide sheet had never been meant to carry passengers.

Unlike Calamity, Belle had not changed clothes, but wore a blanket over the outfit she had worn the previous night, or rather ended the fight in. She left the possum belly and groaned.

"Whooee!" Calamity grinned. "That's a right fetching perfume you're wearing, Belle gal."

"*Eau de* buffalo chips they call it," Belle replied. "The sooner I have a bath and change, the happier I'll be."

"Take the wagon across, Calamity," Mark ordered. "Then I'll ride circle while you both have a bath."

"Yo!" Calamity replied. "Are you riding over, Belle?"

"Not me. I'm going straight in."

That night Calamity and Belle looked much better as they sat around the campfire. They had bathed and combed the tangles out of their hair at the river, and Belle put on a black shirt, a pair of jeans and dainty high-heeled riding boots collected from her trunk which Mark brought to the wagon from the hotel in the small hours of the morning.

"How about coming into Hays with me, Belle?" Calamity asked. "You'll have to pick up a horse."

"That's not a bad id—"

"Just sit right where you are!" a voice interrupted, coming from the blackness beyond the fire. "We've got you under our guns."

Sitting down, Mark could not have reached his guns quick enough to do anything other than get himself killed. Calamity's hip hurt from some part of the fight and she had removed her gunbelt; it lay just too far for her to reach it. Closer lay her blacksnake whip, but she knew better than make a move for it until the person on whom she meant to use it came into range. Belle had her vanity bag hanging from her wrist, but she doubted if she could get her Manhattan out fast enough to give the others a chance.

Soskin and his two men prowled forward into the firelight, their guns in their hands.

"Stay still, Counter," Soskin ordered. "We want Belle."

"You won't get her," Calamity replied, and started to rise.

"Stay down, Calamity!" growled Soskin. "I ain't the sort to worry about shooting a woman, especially one who can handle a gun like you can."

"Do it, Calam!" Belle snapped. "He means what he says."

All the time the others spoke, Mark watched for a chance, but it did not come. While Soskin and his men would have made one of the big-name outlaws retch, they knew enough about the basic details of their trade to avoid giving chances to the people they covered. Faintly, yet distinctly, Mark heard the distant sound of hooves. Two riders at least and it sounded as if they were coming this way. As yet none of the others appeared to have heard the sound. Mark wondered who the approaching travelers

might be. They came from the south, yet they might be
friends of Soskin. Or they could be outlaws who would
throw in with Soskin for a chance at the mythical loot of the
Newton bank job. Even if they were just chance drifters,
Mark did not care to have them horning in, for there would
be no telling which way they would turn if they rode in and
learned that Belle Starr was here.

"You know what we want, Belle?" Soskin asked.

"No."

"Don't play smart!" Varney snorted. "We want the
money you stashed away after the Newton job."

"All of it?"

"Naw," Soskin answered. "We'll play fair with you. Split
it four ways."

"And these two?" Belle went on.

"We'll have to leave 'em so they can't bother us any."

"Sounds a good idea," Belle said quietly, getting to her
feet. "How about Captain Fog and the Ysabel Kid?"

A grin creased Soskin's face. "We circled Elkhorn yesterday and never saw hide nor hair of them. If he is Mark
Counter, he's working alone."

"You could be right at that," Belle purred, then looked at
Calamity. "Sorry about this, Calam, but I just never could
stand playing the losing side."

Sudden fury boiled up inside Calamity and she looked at
Belle. They had been on the best of terms all day, laughing
and joking, discussing the high points of the fight, talking
over their lives. Now Belle was calmly going to side with
the three men who planned to kill them.

"Why you cheap, lousy, double-dealing—!" Calamity began.

Watching Belle move towards Calamity, Mark tensed
slightly. He saw the trio of hardcases were paying more
attention to the girls than to him. Mark did not know what
Belle's game might be, but he guessed something more
than a change of sides lay behind her words.

Stepping towards Calamity, Belle drew back her foot. "I
owe you something from last night," she said.

Just in time Calamity saw Belle's good eye close in a
wink. Then the foot lashed out at her body. Yet it did not

come as fast it might and Calamity had time to shoot up her hands, catch Belle's ankle and twist.

"Get clear of her, Belle!" Soskin bellowed, suddenly seeing the danger.

He saw it a full five seconds too late. Calamity twisted Belle's ankle and caused Belle to stagger. At the same moment Calamity released the ankle, rolled right over and grabbed up her whip.

"It's a trick!" Varney yelled, his gun lining on the staggering Belle.

Several things all started to happen, shattering the group around the fire into sudden and violent action.

Mark flung himself to the left, landing on his side with his right-hand Colt drawn and cocked. Varney's revolver was already lining on Belle when Calamity brought her hand sweeping forward. The lash of the blacksnake whip curled out to wrap around Varney's ankle. Still lying on her side, Calamity heaved back on the whip handle and Varney felt his foot jerk upwards. He fired a shot, but it went harmlessly into the air.

Snarling in a mixture of rage and fear, Carter threw down on Calamity; but Belle had her Manhattan out of her vanity bag's holster. She regained her balance and fired a shot which caught Carter in the shoulder, spun him around and put him out of the fight.

Which left Soskin. Never the quickest of thinkers, the man stood hesitating and trying to decide who to throw lead at first. When dealing with a man like Mark Counter such a show of indecision could prove dangerous. Mark's Colt roared while Soskin's still wavered uncertainly. The gun was batted from Soskin's hand, for Mark had time to take careful aim and did not wish to shoot to kill.

For a moment Varney stood gun in hand, for he had not fallen when Calamity caught his ankle. The whip's lash writhed away, curling behind Calamity as she prepared to strike again. At the same instant Varney found himself facing the barrel of Belle's Manhattan and Mark's Army Colt.

Out drove the whip's lash again, this time with Calamity on her knees and able to get full power behind it. Varney howled as the lash curled around his wrist. He felt as if the bones had been crushed and the gun fell from his hand.

"Which just about ends that," Calamity drawled, shaking free her whip. "Why in hell didn't you wigwag me, Belle gal, let me know what you aimed to do?"

"I reckoned you'd react better without," Belle grinned. "And I was right."

Then they heard the thunder of rapidly approaching hooves.

"Hey, Mark!" yelled a voice. "Any more of them around?"

"Hundreds," Mark called back. "That's why we stood out here all lit by the fire. Come on in and stop that yelling."

Two men rode into the light of the fire. One was a tall, slim, almost babyishly innocent-faced youngster dressed all in black, with a walnut-handled Colt Dragoon at his right side, an ivory-hilted bowie knife at the left. He sat on a huge white stallion with an easy, almost Indian grace, a Winchester rifle in his hands. The other was smaller, not more than five foot six, with dusty blond hair, a handsome though not eye-catching face. Belted at his waist were a pair of white-handled Army Colts, their butts turned for crossdraw. He rode a seventeen-hand paint stallion with two letters burned on its flank: an O and a D, the edge of the O touching the straight line of the D.

"Howdy, Dusty, Lon," Mark greeted. "Wasn't expecting to see you up here."

"We got through our business in Newton early," Dusty Fog replied, swinging from his paint's saddle. "So we reckoned we'd ride up and find out how you were doing."

"Which looks like you're doing all right," the Kid went on, tossing a leg over the saddlehorn and dropping from his white stallion.

Calamity stared at the Rio Hondo gun wizard, Dusty Fog, for a long moment. It seemed Mark had told the truth when he claimed Dusty Fog was a small man. After knowing Dusty for only a few minutes, she never again thought of him as being small.

"What started all this?" Dusty asked. "We saw the fire and rode over to ask if we could camp the night. Saw you were in a tight spot, but you handled it before we reached you."

While Calamity patched up Carter's arm, Mark told

Dusty everything. The small Texan threw a look at Belle, then to where Calamity stood working on, and cursing, the groaning man. From the look of the girls, it had been some fight, yet they appeared to be friendly enough.

"So they wanted you to show them where the loot of the Newton bank job is hidden, Belle," he said. "How'd they plan to get you there?"

"We brought Wicker's hoss along. It's with our'n out on the range," Soskin replied.

"Go and find them, Lon," Dusty said, then turned his attention to the three hardcases. "That would have taken some doing, collecting the money."

"How d'you mean?" asked Soskin sullenly.

"The marshal in Newton isn't as dumb as the sheriff," Dusty explained. "He didn't like some of the signs about the holdup. So he watched the teller, caught him boarding the stage out of town, one that connected with the over-land route to the south. The teller had a nice carpetbag, with thirty thousand dollars inside."

"*What!*" Soskin yelped.

"Sure. When the gang spooked, they dropped the bag with the money in it. So the clerk picked it up, hid it and then gave the alarm."

"And the sheriff's posse shot four men for nothing," Belle said quietly.

"Sure," Dusty agreed. "Then the story about a girl being with the gang came out. Maybe the sheriff was just trying to justify the killings, maybe he believed what he heard. Anyway he put out the dodger on you, Belle, and the story that you had hidden the loot got out."

"Four men died," Belle said quietly. "A bank teller takes a chance and grabs the loot they dropped, and they died."

"Five counting Framant," Calamity Jane put in.

"I wouldn't say that, Calam," Mark drawled. "What killed Framant was the bounty on Belle Starr's scalp."

2

THE CODE OF
THE MOUNTAIN MEN

Mark Counter had been trail boss and brought in a thousand head of long-horned O.D. Connected beef to the town of Brownsville. As a drive it could hardly be compared with running three thousand head up the great interstate trails to the Kansas railroads, but it had had its moments. Enough of them to make Mark grateful that he had Johnny Wade along with him as segundo.

Normally Dusty Fog would have been the trail boss and Mark the segundo, but Dusty and the Ysabel Kid were handling a chore for Ole Devil in the town of Holbrock,* and could not make the drive. Not that Ole Devil had need or cause to worry, for Mark was a master hand with cattle and delivered the herd safely. Now, with the buyer's certified bank draft in the special pocket let into the top of his left Justin boot, Mark was free to have a celebration in the Texas seaport before he and Johnny attended to some private business.

"You should see the place, Mark," Johnny said enthusiastically as they walked towards a saloon away from the dock area. "I was up there for three months last year before I came back to the O.D. Connected. It sure was a swell lil

* Told in *The Half-Breed* by J. T. Edson.

spread, and I can make it grow. Never thought Uncle Zeke would leave it to me, though."

"We'll ride up there and look it over comes the morning," Mark replied.

Johnny was a good hand with cattle and had ridden for the O.D. Connected for almost three years, except for brief spells when he wandered off to see what the rest of the world looked like. However, an uncle had died and left him a small ranch up in the San Vegas hills about fifty miles from Brownsville.

With his characteristic generosity, Ole Devil sent Johnny as segundo on the drive, which gave him extra pay that he could use, and told Mark to go out to the ranch with Johnny and see him settled in on it.

"The Last Battle Saloon," Johnny grinned. "It's as good as any, I'd say. Well, I've bought my supplies, hired me a rig to tote 'em. Now I want to howl."

"We'll go in and howl, then," Mark agreed.

The saloon was one of the better places in Brownsville and drew its customers from a cross section of the town's residents and visitors. Cowhands gathered at tables; blue-clad soldiers mingled with both U.S. Navy and merchant sailors; dockworkers and townsmen rubbed elbows. It could be an explosive mixture when the whisky flowed free, but at this early hour of the evening all seemed quiet and peaceable enough. The faro layout, the chuck-a-luck and blackjack tables all had clients and the wheel of fortune drew a small crowd.

"Not for me," Johnny drawled. "There's no hope in bucking the house percentage in a game."

"Let's try the poker game then," Mark replied. "And let's get sat in on it afore those two gals by the bar come over and eat us."

"What a way to die," grinned Johnny, throwing a glance at the pair of painted saloon girls who looked them over with predatory gaze.

The girls' interest was understandable, for every woman in the room gave the new arrivals more than just a casual looking over.

Johnny stood six foot one, was handsome with curly black hair and a neatly trimmed black mustache. He wore good range clothes and had the build to set them off. Around his waist hung a gunbelt, a matched brace of walnut-handled 1860 Army Colts butt forward in the low Cavalry draw holsters.

In any company Johnny might be expected to catch the eye, for he had wide shoulders, a slim waist, and a great muscular development which most men might have envied.

However, Johnny stood two inches shorter than Mark and Mark possessed even wider shoulders and greater muscle development, as well as being even more handsome. All in all, it had been a long time, if ever, since two more eye-catching, female-attracting men walked into the Last Battle Saloon.

Before the two girls could cross the room and reach them, Mark and Johnny walked to the table where a poker game was in progress.

"Is there room for players, gents?" Johnny asked.

"Settle in and get your feet wet," the tall, slim, well-dressed gambler replied, waving a hand towards the empty chairs. "Game's straight stud, no dealer's choice, no wild cards—and no limit."

"Then she's the game for me. How about you, Mark?"

"Three things I never could stand are dealer's choice, wild cards and a limit. Let's sit a spell and take instruction in how it's done."

None of the four players in the game raised any objection to Mark or Johnny sitting in. The gambler's warning about the lack of a limit had told the cowhands what to expect. They were grown men and as such ought to know whether they could afford to sit in and play under those conditions.

Mark could afford to play in the game. An eccentric maiden aunt left all her money to him when she died and the greater part of the money lay on deposit to him in the Polveroso City Bank back in Rio Hondo County.

While not being rich, Johnny had managed to save some of his pay—a thing that came as a surprise to all who knew him—and had drawn his savings from the bank before leaving to help on the trail drive. So, even after buying supplies for his ranch, he could afford to chance a few hands of stud even in a no limit game. If worse came to worst, he had the deeds to the ranch with which to cover his losses. Not that Johnny wanted to lose the place. He was a cowhand, a top hand at his work, but like most cowhands he tended to live for the moment and let the future take care of itself.

As he sat at the table, Mark studied his fellow players. He knew the gambler to be honest, though obviously an expert at the game or he could not make a living gambling. The man at the gambler's right looked like a senior teller at a bank, or maybe in the county offices. He was fat, stodgy looking, yet he gave the impression he knew the time of day when it came to playing stud poker. To the fat man's right sat a leathery old Army sergeant, short, stocky and tanned to the color of old oak. Nothing about him suggested he would be a rabbit in the game.

That left the fourth player. He sat hunched in a chair facing Mark. A peaked uniform hat rested on the back of his head. His face looked harsh, weather-beaten, and the nose bore testimony that the glass of liquor on the table before him was not the first, nor the thousandth, drink he had ever taken. In dress he looked like an officer of a boat, either master of a small trading craft, or a mate on some larger vessel. The butt of what appeared to be an Adams revolver showed in his waistband. His white shirt looked dirty, the string tie unfastened. His white trousers were tucked into heavy seaboots. All in all he looked as mean as hell and, while not drunk, carried enough of that sickly smelling liquor to slow down his perceptions.

Behind the seaman stood a young woman and at first glance Mark dismissed her as one of the saloon workers. She stood only about five foot two and her mass of long black hair hung down well below her shoulders. It framed a pretty face, a face tanned almost as brown as a Mexican's. She had dark eyes, almost Oriental in appearance, this was emphasized by her rather high cheekbones and the clothes she wore. Mark had seen the style of dress before, on Chinese girls in cathouses at the end-of-trail towns, or in Quiet Town while he served as a deputy under Dusty Fog there just after the War between the States. The dress was shiny material, green in color, fastened high to the neck and slit from hem to thigh. Yet the girl did not look Chinese. Oriental maybe, but no Chinese ever had skin that color and very few showed a round, firm bosom such as forced against the material of the dress. Her arms were bare, brown and undecorated by any of the jewelry a dance-hall or saloon girl usually sported.

"This's Ben Goff," the gambler introduced, waving a hand to the fat man, "Sarge Killet of the 12th Infantry and the Cap'n. Gents, meet Mark Counter from the O.D. Connected and—?"

Under other circumstances it would have been regarded as a breach of range etiquette to ask such a question. However, it could be asked in the informal setting of a card game and the one questioned did not have to give his correct name.

"Johnny Wade," Johnny finished for the gambler, looking at the girl behind the seaman with interest.

"She don't work here, cowboy," the seaman growled. "She's mine."

Not by a flicker of her face did the girl show any interest in either Johnny's frankly admiring glance, or the man's words.

"No offense, mister," Johnny replied quietly.

Mark, the gambler, the soldier and the fat man exchanged glances. All knew that when a cowhand called a man mister after being introduced he did not like the man. Not that they blamed Johnny, the seaman's comment had been uncalled for. The young cowhand had done no more than look at the girl and could not be expected to know she did not work in the saloon.

Riffling the cards, Packer, the gambler, placed them down for Mark to cut.

"Cut 'em light, lose all night," Mark drawled. "Flip 'em out and let's see who's going to take it from me."

Out flipped the cards, the first face down and then the second exposed.

"And it's the ace to bet," Packer remarked.

"I'll open it with ten," Johnny, who held the ace, replied.

From the start two things became clear to Mark: that the standard of play would be high; and that the seaman was out of his league in such a game. So would Johnny have been, for he played the way he lived, on impulse more than sound judgment.

Where the other three closed a hand that did not show firm hope of being worthwhile, Johnny and the seaman clung to it, staying in the pot and hoping for a last card miracle to save the day. This was not, and never had been, good poker, as the seaman found out to his cost. Johnny might have found it also, but he seemed to be in the middle of one of those flows of luck which made gambling so fascinating to most people. Time after time he would sit with poor hands, betting on them and the last card brought off a winner, or he would run a bluff and scoop the pot.

The seaman was the heavy loser. None of the others took such chances and held their own, or lost a little, knowing the law of averages would in the end crack the run of luck.

After the game had been going for an hour, Johnny glanced at the girl. She still stood behind the seaman's chair and he had not given her as much as a glance as he played his hands and drank glass after glass of rum without it showing any effect.

While the fat man shuffled the cards, Johnny came to his feet, fetching a chair from another table.

"Here, ma'am," he said, putting the chair behind the girl. "Have a seat."

Swinging around, the seaman glared up at Johnny, his drink-reddened face going a shade or two deeper colored. For a long moment he studied Johnny's big frame, read the challenge in the cowhand's eyes and shrugged.

"Sit down!" he growled.

Obediently the girl sank into the chair, sitting primly on the edge of it and folding her hands on her lap. She gave Johnny a look of silent gratitude as he returned to his seat and took up his cards.

A few hands went by and the seaman grew more surly with each one. His losses had been heavy and his consumption of rum almost continuous. Fumbling into his coat's inside pocket, he took out a stiff white sheet of paper and tossed it towards Johnny with an angry gesture.

"Here, the bill of sale for Jaya, give me two hundred on it!"

"Two hundred?" Johnny replied, wondering why the man would offer his ship for such a small sum.

"She's worth it."

"Reckon she might be to you," Johnny agreed, then he shrugged. "Sure, two hundred it is."

Easy come, easy go, that was Johnny. He had no use for a ship, but could always let the seaman redeem the bill of sale after the game. Way Johnny saw it, a man who had suffered from such stinking luck in the game deserved a chance to break even.

"Let's call this the last hand, shall we?" the fat man asked, watching Mark riffle the cards.

None of the others objected, although the seaman muttered something under his breath. The other players in the game, poker addicts though they were, did not like the seaman's attitude enough to want to continue playing with him. All had played enough poker to know such a man in his present condition might make trouble that could end up in gunplay. So, rather than wind up with a corpse and cartridge affair, they would break up the game.

"I'll do it!" the seaman growled as Mark passed the cards to Johnny for the cut.

Under the rules of poker any player could ask to cut the cards before the deal. Yet the seaman's attitude annoyed Mark, brought a frown of disapproval to the gambler's face, an angry grunt from the soldier and a worried look to the fat townsman. Johnny's hands clenched, but he caught a warning headshake from Mark and kept his thoughts to himself. Only he sure hoped that loudmouth made some remark after the game. It would give Johnny the pleasure to bounce that sullen yahoo around the room.

Out sailed the cards, landing face down on the table, followed by the next turned face up for all to see. The seaman peeked at his hole card, the king of hearts and he had the ace of spades showing. Across the table Johnny sat with the four of hearts showing.

"I'll open," growled the seaman.

Mark threw his cards in, the three of clubs and nine of diamonds did not have enough possibility of improvement to make it worth his while staying in on them. The others stayed in and Mark dealt them their third cards. The seaman caught the queen of diamonds and Johnny received the nine of hearts. After seeing the card he received, the fat man followed the other players out, leaving the pot between Johnny and the seaman.

On receiving a ten of spades, the seaman pushed up the betting and Johnny drew the seven of hearts. Again they bet and the last cards flipped to them from the deck. Nobody spoke, but every eye went first to the jack of clubs before the seaman and the six of hearts which lay on Johnny's hand.

"Ace to bet," the gambler said quietly.

Indecision showed on the seaman's face, a trickle of sweat ran down his brow and he brushed it aside. Although he held as high a straight as a man could get, one little heart in the hole would give Johnny a flush; and that would beat any straight no matter how high.

Having seen how Johnny's luck ran through the game, the seaman felt uneasy. Nothing in the young cowhand's face or attitude showed any hint of alarm, or sign that he might be running a bluff.

"I'll check," the seaman said.

"Then she's loose for a hundred," Johnny answered.

Once again the man paused and studied the cards. He lifted his face to look at Johnny. The other players stayed silent, waiting to see the outcome of the game.

Slowly the seaman reached out a hand. He looked at the money before him and gave an angry scowl.

"I'm out!" he snarled and folded his cards.

With a broad grin, Johnny scooped in the pot and thrust back his chair. He looked at the other players.

"Drinks are on me, gents," he said. "Let's head for the bar."

All but the seaman rose to accept Johnny's invitation. They left the cards on the table just as when the deal finished. The seaman leaned over and lifted up Johnny's hole card. A snarl of fury came from the man's lips. He dropped the two of spades face up on the table. Johnny had run a bluff and the seaman knew he had fallen for it.

Coming to his feet and throwing his chair over, the seaman drew the Adams revolver from his waistband.

"Look out!"

The girl had not moved from her chair, nor had her eyes left Johnny since he accepted the bill of sale from the seaman. Now she came to her feet and screamed a warning.

It came almost too late. The Adams's bullet missed Johnny by inches as he started to turn, thrusting the gambler and fat man aside and twisting his right hand palm out to hook around its gun butt.

Mark also turned, saw the seaman and acted. Faster than Johnny moved, Mark brought out his left hand Colt, his right hand shooting out to send the old soldier staggering to safety. Flame ripped from the barrel and the seaman reeled back under the impact of the lead. He still held his gun and tried to shoot, swinging the Adams in Mark's direction. It gave Mark no choice. He fired again, sending the bullet into the man's head and tumbling him in a lifeless heap on the floor.

The girl screamed, twisting away from the sight and standing with her hands clenched at her sides. Everybody in the room swung around, preparing to take cover. Smoke dribbled up from Mark's Colt and Johnny thrust his weapon back into its holster.

"Thanks, Mark," he said. "Looks like the feller saw I'd run a bluff on him and didn't like it."

"Sure looks that way," Mark replied. "I figured you hadn't filled the flush at all."

"I hadn't. Reckoned to give him a chance to win his boat back. I'd best go thank the lady, she saved me for sure."

"Go to it," Mark answered. "I'll send for the marshal."

Crossing the room, Johnny halted by the girl and looked down at her. She turned a frightened face to him.

"Thanks for the warning, ma'am," he said. "I'm sorry about what happened to your man."

"He is not my man," she replied. "You are."

"*Me?*" Johnny asked, his voice rising a shade. "How'd you make that out?"

"My name is Jaya Hara. You won me from the captain. I saw him give you the papers."

The town marshal arrived and heard the details of the shooting, declared it to be self-defense and that no action need be taken against Mark. In Texas at that time people took the sensible view that a man could defend his life, or the life of a friend, even to the extent of killing an aggressor should it be necessary. Mark had not sought a fight, but he shot to prevent the seaman killing Johnny and the law rightly found no fault in his actions.

Leaving the marshal to attend to the removal of the body, Mark crossed the room and joined Johnny at the bar. The little girl stood with Johnny and from the expression on Johnny's face, he was trying to explain something to her.

"I can't own you, Jaya," Johnny was saying as Mark joined them.

"You do," she replied and Mark could detect a faint accent in her speech. "The captain sold me to you. I saw him."

"Mark," Johnny groaned, turning to his big *amigo*, "tell Jaya that a man can't sell a gal to anybody."

"Let's get out of here first," Mark replied. "Like the marshal says, that feller might have friends, and he doesn't want a shooting war between the cowhands and sailors."

Turning, Mark headed for the door. Johnny watched him go, then followed, for he could see the wisdom in the marshal's suggestion. If the dead man had friends they might come back looking for revenge. Johnny and Mark could handle their guns and take care of their end in any man's fight, but the sailors would tend to side with their kind. This in turn would bring the cowhands in to help Mark and Johnny and could blow the whole town apart at the seams.

"Give me my bag, please," Jaya said to the bartender. "The smaller one."

"Sure," he replied, bending to lift a canvas duffel bag from the floor. "How about the other one?"

"I do not want it," she answered, swinging the bag to her shoulder and hurrying across the room after the departing men.

"What were you saying in there?" Mark asked as he and Johnny left the saloon and walked along the sidewalk.

"That lil gal, Jaya she says her name is, she reckons I bought her off that sailor."

At that moment Johnny sensed rather than heard the girl

and turned towards her. Mark also swung around, looking at the bag the girl carried.

"What in hell?" Johnny snapped. "Look, gal, I don't own you."

"Yes you do. You have paper—"

"Durn the paper!" Johnny interrupted. "I'll give you the—"

"Let's get off the street and talk this out!" Mark put in urgently, for a few people were looking in their direction, attracted by Johnny's rising voice.

"Yeah, we'd better," Johnny replied. "Come on—and give me that durned bag, gal."

Jaya looked at Johnny in surprise as he took the bag from her hand, slung it onto his shoulder and turned to walk away. For the first time her full lips parted in a smile. Her mouth looked just a shade too large for some tastes, but the teeth were firm and even, without the gold filling so many Chinese girls sported. She fell into line behind him and followed on his heels.

Stopping, Johnny looked back at the girl. "Come on up here and walk between Mark and me, gal," he ordered.

"It would not be correct for me to do so," she answered.

"Dad-blast it, gal, this's Texas. You come between us."

Somehow they attracted less attention walking that way, although several people threw knowing looks at them. The looks annoyed Johnny for some reason. On more than one occasion he had escorted a girl through the streets and received the same sort of looks, only then the looks had been justified. This time he had no ulterior motive; and, strangely, the thought of the implied suggestion about Jaya's morals riled him.

On reaching the hotel where they had taken rooms, Johnny went to the reception desk and jerked a thumb toward Jaya. The reception clerk, a plump, pompous dude with spectacles and sideburns, looked at the girl, then turned an indignant face to Johnny.

"This isn't the sort of hotel—!" he began.

"They never are," Johnny replied. "The lady's taking my room and I'm bunking with my *amigo.*"

"Yes?" sniffed the clerk.

"*Yes!*" Johnny barked, his hands slapping palms down on

the desktop and causing the clerk to take a hurried pace to the rear. "Any objections?"

"N—no, sir. None at all!"

Actually the clerk had several objections, but he remembered that the big blond cowhand had appeared to be on friendly terms with the hotel's owner, so kept his views to himself. Besides, he knew cowhands. One wrong word could cause more trouble than the clerk reckoned he could handle.

On reaching the door of his room, Johnny unlocked it and handed the key and her bag to Jaya.

"Say," he said, "do you have any other clothes in that bag?"

"Of course."

"You'd best put another dress on. That one sure attracts attention."

"Yes—may I call you Johnny? I heard your friend call you Johnny."

"Sure you can, Jaya," Johnny replied. "Come give me a knock when you're changed, then we'll go eat."

"You not wanting me to cook for you?" she gasped.

"Not today," Johnny grinned. "Let's say you're on holiday."

"I never had a holiday before," Jaya sighed, opening the room door and stepping inside. "I like belonging to you, Johnny."

Sitting on his bed, Mark grinned at Johnny when the young cowhand entered the room.

"What's amusing you?" Johnny asked. "That's a nice gal there."

"Sure is," Mark agreed. "What're you fixing to do with her?"

"Me?"

"You," Mark agreed. "She reckons you own her."

Johnny flung his hat on the small dressing table angrily. "You know that isn't possible, Mark."

"Why sure," Mark agreed. "I know it, you know it. But does *she* know it?"

"I'll explain it to her while we're eating," Johnny drawled. "It's allus easy to explain things to a gal when she's full fed."

At that moment the door of the room opened and Jaya entered. She wore a different dress. The sight of it lifted Johnny out of his chair and even Mark, who reckoned to be blasé about females, stared.

From waist to ankles the dress looked normal, no slit through which shapely legs could peek seductively, the sort of thing any good woman in town would wear. Above the waist—well, it would raise a dead Indian, if one had been close at hand. The material clung so tight that it seemed molded to her and left her arms and shoulders bare, apart from the two straps. The neckline of the dress had been cut down lower than even a dance-hall girl in a wide-open town would chance wearing, and showed that Jaya wore nothing but the dress.

"I have changed my dress as you say," Jaya announced unnecessarily.

"Land-sakes, gal!" Johnny gasped. "Is that the only one you have?"

"No, I have others, but they are smaller than this one."

Under different circumstances Johnny would not have cared how scantily a girl dressed. Yet somehow he felt differently about Jaya. She looked so small and helpless, if a man kept his eyes on her face. He did not feel she should dress in anything so revealing when men could see her.

"Go put a coat on," he said. "I'll take you to the store and buy you a couple of dresses."

Left alone in the room, Mark lay back on his bed and grinned up at the roof. He knew Johnny very well and had been surprised at the cowhand's behavior towards the girl. With any other girl, or any other girl he had met in a saloon, Johnny would never have thought of handing over his room, or worried about how she dressed. Yet he had taken the little girl in and was spending money to buy her clothes more suited to the ideas people had about how a young woman ought to dress.

Maybe the chance meeting would have its use, Mark thought. While Johnny was a top hand with cattle, ready to work all hours of the day and night, or give his lifeblood for the brand he worked for, he never accepted responsibility. He would need to if he hoped to make the ranch he inherited pay. What Johnny needed was a steadying influence, a wife—but would that girl make him the right kind of wife?

When Johnny returned, he presented Jaya clad in a gingham dress of modest, conventional pattern. A parcel he carried contained two more, and various articles of underclothing the storekeeper's wife insisted Jaya would need, for her scanty wardrobe did not contain any such luxuries.

"Let's go eat and talk things out," Mark suggested.

Over the meal, with Jaya attracting little attention in her new clothes, the girl told her story.

Jaya was born in a seaport on the Siam coast, although Mark had only a vague idea, and Johnny none at all, where this might be. Her father had been a German trader, her mother a Javanese dancing girl. Not that her father had been a very successful trader, the girl admitted, in fact he spent so much time drinking that he rarely had any business to support an ever-growing family.

Four years ago her father needed money and sold her to the man Mark killed, the captain of a small trading ship. From the calm way Jaya spoke of the matter, it did not appear to be an unusual transaction in her homeland. The captain kept her on the ship as his cook and servant, strangely he had treated her as nothing worse—probably because he planned to sell her to some brothel keeper when she matured and knew he would gain a higher price that way. Then for some reason not unconnected with piracy, but into which Jaya did not go, the man sailed for the United States. He brought his ship around the tip of South America to make for the eastern seaboard rather than chance recognition on the West Coast. On arrival at Brownsville, the captain had been in urgent need of money. He brought the girl ashore to try to sell her, however, the card game at the Last Battle Saloon gave Jaya a stay and Mark wrote a finish to the man's plan.

"I did not want to be what he would sell me for," she finished, looking at Johnny with her luminous black eyes and pleading that he believe her. "I am good girl. I cook good, mend clothes or make them. I am strong, work very hard for you all the time, Johnny."

"But I don't own you," Johnny groaned.

"You do. You have the papers."

"Dang the papers!" Johnny yelled, then dropped his voice. "They don't mean a thing. You can go any time you want."

"I not want to go," she said. "You good man, you own me. I not leave you."

Nor would any amount of arguing shake the girl. Mark tried to help out by explaining the impossibility of Johnny owning her, but she brushed aside every suggestion that she was free.

"Blast it, Mark!" Johnny growled as they followed the girl upstairs after the meal. "How do—say, I've an idea. Let's me and you go out and have us a time. That way she'll see that I don't care."

"I'll go along with you," Mark replied. "It may work."

Not until they had reached the saloon nearest to the hotel did Johnny remember he had left his saddle, bedroll and war bag in the hotel room that he loaned to Jaya. Yet he did not worry for his every instinct told him his belongings would be safe.

It had been Johnny's intention to get drunk, which he did, then pick a gal as unlike Jaya as he could find and take her back to the hotel with him. That ought to show Jaya he wanted no part of her. He even had the right girl picked out, a large, buxom blond beauty who would make two of Jaya in size and heft. The girl would have agreed to Johnny's proposal, but did not get a chance.

Just as Johnny started to walk towards the girl and suggest they make a night of it, he seemed to see another face before him. One with a mass of long black hair, dainty, pretty features and luminous, yet sad, black eyes. Suddenly Johnny wanted no part of the big blonde.

Instead he drank more than he meant to. Whisky never made Johnny aggressive. The only effect it had on him was to make him sleepy. After a time Mark steered Johnny back to the hotel. In their room Johnny gravely thanked Mark, shaking his hand and telling him that he was the best damned *amigo* a man ever had. Then Johnny undressed and headed for his blankets which lay on the floor at the side of the room. Mark had done some drinking himself, though not as much as Johnny, and certainly not enough to make him lose his memory. Yet he could not remember

Johnny bringing the bedroll into the room and spreading it out ready for use.

Mark was still thinking about the matter of Johnny's bedroll when he went to sleep. Light sleeper though Mark usually was, he did not hear the door open. A dark shape entered, spent a few minutes in the room and left as silently as it came.

"Where in hell's my clothes?"

Daylight streamed in through the room's window as Mark woke to Johnny's wail of anger. Sitting up in bed, Mark looked across the room to where Johnny sat on his blankets and stared around the room.

"Is this your fool idea of a joke?" Johnny growled, seeing Mark watching him. "Come on, Mark, where in h—"

His words died off as the room's door opened to admit Jaya carrying a cloth-covered tray. Johnny let out a startled yelp and ducked under his blankets, drawing them around his naked torso.

"I have brought you coffee," the girl said, setting the tray on a chair. "Shall I bring your breakfast to you?"

"Huh?" Johnny gasped. "Hey—no! And you shouldn't come in here like this, Jaya. I'm not dressed."

"I will fetch your clothes," she replied and left the room.

An amazed-looking face stared at Mark as the door closed behind the girl. Mark could not hold down his grin, for he had never seen Johnny so completely at a loss for words.

"D—did she—?" Johnny croaked.

"Not that I know of," Mark grinned. "I never saw her when we got back here. You undressed yourself and went to sleep, like a baby when its mother sings a lullaby."

"How'd you like me to sing you a lul—"

Once more Johnny's words died off as he stared at Jaya. The girl came into the room carrying a neat pile of clothes. Johnny's Stetson, freshly brushed and with the silver conchas of its band gleaming, lay on top of the pile. His spare shirt, undershirt and underpants, all clean and pressed, his jeans, tidied up after their wear, and boots showing an unaccustomed shine, completed the girl's load. Placing the clothes down, Jaya reached into one of the boots and took out a clean, darned pair of socks which certainly had not been clean or darned when Johnny last saw them.

"I have packed your old clothes away to be washed when I have time," she said. "Can I—"

"No!" Johnny yelped as if the words had been stung out of him by a bee. He held the blankets tighter to him. "I can dress myself."

A gentle smile played on the girl's lips.

"I only wanted to know if I could pour out the coffee for you."

Mark grinned and spoke up. "I'll take a cup, if I can, ma'am."

Whisking the cloth from the tray, Jaya poured out two cups of coffee and looked at Johnny.

"How do you like it?" she asked.

"Black and sweet," he replied, sounding dazed.

"I will remember in the future," she promised.

Although Johnny thought up some comment about her having no need to remember, he did not use it. The aroma of the cup of coffee Jaya handed to him made him forget the speech.

"No hotel cook ever threw up Arbuckle's like this," Mark drawled, accepting the cup Jaya carried to him after serving Johnny.

"I made it myself," the girl answered. "Please get dressed now so you can go and eat the breakfast I have cooked for you."

"Sure, Jaya gal," Johnny replied. "Just you go and let us dress."

Not until he was dressing did Johnny realize his wallet and money belt had been among his clothes. Before he could mention this to Mark, he found them under his pillow. Johnny, who had known enough saloon girls to have few illusions left, never even thought of checking that the money was intact.

"Where in hell did the bed come from?" he asked.

Mark rose, and began to dress before he answered.

"Jaya must have brought it in for you. What're you going to do about her?"

"I don't know," Johnny admitted. "I can't just turn the

gal loose down here. She'd never get by. I reckon I'll take her up to the ranch until she knows her way around."

"Why not marry her?" Mark replied.

Johnny was climbing into his pants as Mark spoke. He stopped with one leg in the air, twisted around and almost fell.

"Marry!" he howled. "Mark, you-all been falling on your lil pumpkin head too many times. Why in hell should I get married?"

"Why not?" Mark countered. "You're all set to settle down and be a rancher. So, you're going to need a woman to run the house."

"Nah!" Johnny snorted. "A gal'd just be a drag to me. I'll take her up to the spread, if she wants to come. But when she knows her way around, waal, I'll stake her to wherever she wants to go."

There the matter rested for the time being. The two men washed and shaved, finished dressing and went downstairs to eat a good breakfast served to them by Jaya. She seemed to be surprised when Johnny insisted she join them, and sat watching him with smiling lips and happy eyes.

Before they left the hotel Mark saw its owner, a friend from his Army days. He learned that Jaya had worked until long after he and Johnny went to bed, at washing Johnny's clothes, sewing tears and replacing missing buttons, darning his socks and cleaning his boots and hat.

Mark did not tell Johnny of his findings. He paid the hotel bill and they took Jaya to collect the hired wagon, then drive to the store and load the ranch's supplies.

"You stack and I'll load," Mark told Johnny on reaching the store.

"Any way you want, *amigo*," Johnny replied.

Neither of the men noticed Jaya, who had ridden alongside Johnny on the wagon box, climb down and walk onto the sidewalk. The girl followed Mark into the store and watched him pick up a sack of potatoes, sling it on his shoulder and stroll out of the door with no more apparent effort than a kid toting a bag of candy.

"I thought I'd tote all the heavy stuff out first," he told Johnny who took the sack from him.

"Any way you—" Johnny began, then glanced at the store's door. He stood up fast, his eyes bulging wide open. "Great blistering horned toad! Will you take a look at that?"

Swinging around, Mark saw what had startled Johnny. The sight rocked him back on his heels too.

Jaya came through the door and across the sidewalk, toting a heavy sack of sugar on her back. She walked forward, bowing under the weight, but kept moving with it.

To his credit, Johnny reached the sidewalk even before Mark. He sprang over the side of the wagon and took the sack from the girl's back.

"Land-sakes, gal!" he grunted. "What're you trying to do, kill yourself?"

"It was not heavy," she replied.

Johnny could have given her an argument about that. The sack *was* heavy, far heavier than he would have believed the girl's small figure capable of bearing.

Coming from the store, the owner looked worriedly to where Johnny stood heaving the sack onto the wagon.

"I'm sorry, friend," he said. "The lady came in and asked me which was your gear. I showed her, and next thing I knowed she'd picked that sack up and toted it outside. I never even thought she could heft it from the floor."

"And she'd best not heft any more," Johnny replied grimly.

"I do not please you, Johnny?" Jaya gasped, looking worried.

"Sure you do," he replied with a grin and gently laid a hand on her head to ruffle her hair. "Only there's no call for you to go hefting the heavy stuff around. You lend a hand with the lighter gear if you like."

By the time the wagon was loaded, Jaya had proved she knew how to stack a load, spread a tarpaulin over it and lash the tarp home securely. She showed embarrassment when Johnny pressed some money into her hand and told her to go buy a present.

"Man'd be a fool to let a gal like her slip through his fingers," Mark drawled as he and Johnny watched Jaya skip lightly into the store.

"Likely," Johnny agreed. "Only I'm not the marrying kind."

Normally Mark would have accepted, probably applauded his friend's decision to avoid the bonds of matrimony. However, on this occasion he figured he should break his rule. Johnny needed a good wife, and Jaya showed signs of being a better girl for the job than the sort Johnny would pick given first and free choice of the remuda. Jaya needed a husband, there were too few ways a woman could earn a decent living in the West; and Johnny would make a good husband once he settled in to the idea. Only if Mark knew Johnny, and he reckoned he did, he didn't figure the cowhand would want him handing out advice on the subject of matrimony. More so when thinking of Mark's views on the subject as it affected him personally.

There was one way to make Johnny see the light though; and Mark reckoned he was just the boy to do it.

Jaya used the money Johnny gave her to buy a Stetson hat. When she sat by his side on the wagon box, her eagerness to have pleased him by the purchase started Johnny worrying. The last thing he wanted was for her to get too attached to him. Sure, she was a great little gal, but it was just that Johnny did not think he could make a marrying man.

"Pass it down this way, Jaya," Mark said, riding his blood-bay stallion at the side of the wagon. "I'll shape it Texas style for you."

Glancing hopefully at Johnny, who pretended to be too busy handling the reins and making sure his big dun horse followed the wagon, to the tail of which its reins were fastened, Jaya handed Mark the hat.

"See you bought a good hat," Mark went on, altering the Stetson's crown to meet the dictates of Texas fashion. "It's always worth the money."

Johnny looked towards the girl, now facing Mark and engrossed in his words of wisdom on the subject of hats. Having seen Mark in action around the ladies before, Johnny felt a hint of relief. He did not forget how Mark cut the ground from under his feet one time with the best-looking girl in a Newton saloon. From the way things looked, Johnny reckoned Mark to be using the same technique with Jaya.

"Good ole Mark," he thought. "You're sure taking that lil gal off my back."

Then another thought struck him. In a way he was responsible for Jaya. If he had not brought her out here there would be no need for Mark to take her off his back. What about after Mark got the gal interested? Johnny knew Mark too well to reckon anything more serious than a flirtation could come with Jaya. So what would she do after Mark rode on?

For the first time Johnny began to think of Jaya's many good points. He also decided he had best try to stop her becoming too involved with Mark. Not that he cared one way or the other, of course, but he did not want to see that innocent little gal get hurt.

So Johnny tried to regain Jaya's attention. Woman-like, Jaya's feelings had been hurt by Johnny's apparent indifference to her choice of hats—when she made the choice because she felt it would please him and instead of buying some cheap, rather gaudy jewelry which attracted her. So she intended to make Johnny suffer a little for his indifference.

For the rest of the day, while they traveled across the range heading towards the San Vegas hill country, Johnny tried to get into the conversation which went on between Mark and the girl. He met with little success.

When they made camp for the night, Mark allowed Johnny to slip in and show Jaya how to handle the unhitching and care of the wagon horse. The girl cooked a meal for them and they prepared to settle down for the night.

"You can use my pillow and blankets, Jaya," Mark said.

"There's a spare blanket on the wagon," Johnny put in. "We'll make Jaya a bed under the wagon and we'll sleep by the fire."

"Where else?" Mark replied.

He found that Johnny spread his bedroll on the side of the fire nearest to the wagon. Nor did Johnny go to sleep until he saw and heard the rhythmic breathing by which he assumed that Mark had already settled down for the night. Mark looked across the fire at the now sleeping Johnny and a grin came to his lips. Turning over, Mark drew his blankets up higher. It looked like old Johnny was beginning to point the way Mark wanted him to go.

They moved on at dawn, after a good breakfast and some of Jaya's coffee. What that girl could do with Arbuckle's coffee had to be tasted to be believed. Johnny had always liked good coffee and he could not remember any that tasted just as good to his palate as the kind Jaya made.

Once more Johnny missed his chance. Mark's praise of the coffee brought a smile to Jaya's lips and she turned to Johnny.

"Do you like it?" she asked.

"Huh? Sure, it's all right."

Straight off Johnny could have cursed himself. With an annoyed toss of her head, Jaya turned and carried the coffeepot away, pouring a good cup full that Johnny would have liked over the fire's flames.

Once more Mark monopolized the conversation with the girl and Johnny scowled to himself, concentrating on driving. His few attempts to say anything found the girl attentive, but each time Mark cut him out.

Towards sundown they came into sight of the ranch buildings and Johnny brought the wagon to a halt. He did not notice that Mark dropped back and left him alone with the girl and the view.

"There it is, Jaya," Johnny said, a note of pride in his voice.

"I think it is beautiful, Johnny," she replied and her voice sent a thrill through him.

Compared with the O.D. Connected's great two-story main building, the house below did not appear very grand. Yet Johnny did not care. After all, he did not own the O.D. Connected but he did own that house down there and a fair slice of the surrounding land.

The house was stoutly made of logs, with a good strong roof over it, glass in the windows and a porch on which a man could sit and rock in the evening while his wife made supper for him. There was a good-sized, well-made barn, a blacksmith's forge, a backhouse and a couple of stoutly constructed pole corrals. His uncle had built to last and it would be long, given reasonable care, before Johnny would need to start rebuilding.

"Let's go take a look inside," Johnny suggested eagerly and the girl, clutching his arm, agreed.

Watching the wagon roll down the slope, Mark smiled. He had not failed to notice how Johnny and Jaya acted. Give them a couple of days, and Johnny a little more of the treatment handed out the last couple of days, and Mark reckoned he could leave his two friends in each other's care.

A pump and empty horse trough stood before the house. Mark swung from his blood bay's saddle and went to the pump, starting to fill the big trough. A woman could likely do her wash in it, or even take a bath on warm days when her man and the help worked the range.

Side by side Jaya and Johnny ran from the wagon, across the porch and to the door. When Johnny's uncle rode into Brownsville for the last time, he had locked the door and taken the key. Apart from the sheriff's deputies checking in once in a while, nobody had been near the house since that day. Johnny unlocked the door and he and Jaya entered.

The house had a simple layout much used in the West. The front consisted of one room, serving as dining room, sitting room, lounge, library combined. It was furnished, the furniture not new, but still in good condition. Three doors led off at the rear, two to bedrooms, one into the kitchen.

The dust of a month of emptiness lay everywhere, but apart from that the place appeared to be untouched.

"Tomorrow," Jaya said, looking around her, "we start to clean everything."

"Whatever you say," Johnny replied.

Mark came into the room, halting and looking around him. Turning, Johnny looked at his *amigo* and grinned, finding it impossible to stay annoyed.

"How'd you like it, Mark?"

"Great. A stout little house with all the furnishings. You've got a good home here, Johnny boy. I'll go tend to the horses, unless Jaya wants another lesson in horse-handling."

"She don't!" Johnny grunted, before the girl could answer. "I want to show her her room—"

On finding her kitchen, Jaya chased Johnny off out to help Mark with the horses while she started the stove and prepared a meal for them. Johnny joined Mark outside and worked in silence, which Mark knew to be unusual for Johnny.

"Jaya says we're starting housecleaning tomorrow," Mark remarked as he turned the harness horse into one of the corrals. "Reckon she's the boss on that end of the spread."

"Reckon she is," Johnny replied. "You figure it'll be all right for you to stay on here, Mark? Ole Devil might have something for you to handle."

"Nope. He told me to take a few days vacation. So I might as well do it up here, lending you a hand. I wonder if Jaya's got everything she needs in the kitchen?"

"I'll go see," Johnny grunted.

Watching Johnny walk away, Mark grinned broadly. He attended to the horses and when finished, walked to the house. Johnny and Jaya appeared to be getting on much better.

"Johnny boy," Mark thought as he joined them at the table, "you've one foot in the hole and the other on a greasy slope. Just a lil mite more pushing and I'll leave you set up for life."

So Mark kept on the pushing. When he wished, he could talk fascinatingly about a number of things. Jaya listened to his descriptions of the prewar South, of Maximilian's court in Mexico; and Johnny sat watching the girl, getting more and more sure that he must protect her from Mark.

Not that Johnny cared about her himself. He just did not want to see her hurt—or so he told himself.

The girl showed off another accomplishment, although not one Johnny approved of her doing in mixed company. From her bundle of belongings, she produced a scanty sleeveless blouse and a skirt which seemed to be made of grass, hanging to her knees. Wearing these, and barefoot, she began to dance. It was a dance like the two men had never seen before, with swaying hips, sensuous writhing body movements.

Johnny felt hot under the collar as she sank to her knees in the dusty room and faced him, leaning her torso back as she writhed and her arms moved gracefully in the pagan dance. He enjoyed every movement of it, but swore she would never again dance like that before another man.

"That is how the native girls dance in the South Sea Islands," she said, rising to her feet. "Did you like?"

"I've never seen better," Mark answered.

"You go put your other dress on now," Johnny put in, for the grass skirt revealed more of the girl's legs than even the Chinese frock had. "You'll catch a cold in that outfit."

Once again Mark could cheerfully have kicked Johnny across the room. The girl wanted his praise, and instead of giving it, telling her how he enjoyed her dance, the durned fool had to make a remark like that.

A very indignant Jaya stormed out of the room, to return wearing the gingham dress. Ignoring Johnny, she began to ask Mark questions about the range, things a woman should know about and which Johnny wished he could be discussing with her.

"It's time we were getting to bed!" he growled, unable to stand it any longer. "You use the bedroom, Jaya. Me 'n' Mark'll bunk down in the barn until we get the place cleaned up."

Not until they had spread their bedrolls in the barn, with Johnny getting between Mark and the door, did the young cowhand speak to his blond *amigo*.

"Take it easy on Jaya, Mark," he said.

"How do you mean?" Mark asked, straight-faced but enjoying every minute of the situation.

"Shucks, she's not used to being around fellers. She might—you—that is—it's—"

"I thought you hadn't any claim on her," Mark drawled.

"I don't have!" Johnny snapped. "It's just that I feel responsible for her after fetching her out here."

"Do, huh?"

"Sure, I do!"

"I'll mind what you say," Mark said calmly. "Now let's get some sleep. We've got a big day ahead of us."

And with that, Mark undressed and climbed into his bed. He went to sleep almost immediately, knowing Johnny was willing himself to stay awake until sure he had nothing to fear.

Dawn brought a fresh problem for Johnny. Jaya came to tell them that she had breakfast ready for them.

"What're you wearing that dress for?" he yelled indignantly, for it was the one into which she had changed at the hotel and which caused him to buy her new clothes.

"I have much work to do," she replied. "It is not good that I should dirty my good clothes."

"Yeah, but—"

Sitting up, Mark looked at the girl and interrupted Johnny's protests.

"Man, you look prettier than a june bug, Jaya," he said.

"Thank you, Mark," she replied. "Johnny thinks I should wear my good dress to work in."

"That'd be real foolish, was you to ask me," Mark drawled.

"Nobody did," Johnny growled.

"I have breakfast ready," Jaya said, in a tone which showed she considered the matter of her dress closed. "Hurry, before it gets cold."

Not even the mood of "to hell with her, let her make a durned fool of herself over him," could last in the face of Jaya's coffee and breakfast. Johnny ate well and even managed to compliment her on her cooking, and her appearance.

With the breakfast over, Jaya gave her orders, and from the way she spoke the men saw they were going to have a hard and busy morning. On leaving the house, Mark removed his shirt and undershirt, putting them with his hat and gunbelt on the wagon box.

"You can't go around like that!" Johnny objected.

"Why not?" Mark replied. "Jaya's been on a ship and likely seen a man's bare chest before now, so why should I get my clothes mussed up?"

"Johnny!" Jaya called, coming to the cabin door. "Will you and Mark come and move the furniture for me?"

"Sure," Johnny replied, stepping hurriedly before Mark in the hope of hiding his naked torso and saving Jaya embarrassment.

"Why don't you take off your shirt too?" she asked. "It will save me some washing."

For a moment Johnny thought of ignoring the advice. Then he thought why the hell should that big blond tub of lard get off showing his physique to Jaya. Maybe Mark was a mite bigger, but Johnny reckoned his own build was not exactly so puny that he need be ashamed to show it off. So he stripped off his shirt and left it, hat and gunbelt with Mark's on the wagon.

Not that Johnny had time to stand around and let Jaya admire his well-developed body. If she noticed it at all, Jaya gave no hint. Instead she had the two men working hard, carrying all the furniture out into the space before the house while she heated water.

"She sure has some go for a lil 'un," Johnny said admiringly, looking towards the house.

"Yep, she sure has," Mark agreed. "Let's go clean out the barn while she does her chores in the house."

Despite all his suspicions of Mark's intentions, Johnny went along with the idea. They heard the sound of scrubbing and Jaya's voice as she sang a song in a lilting tongue neither could understand, but which sounded mighty sweet to a man's ears. It made him think of the way Jaya looked in that frock, or how she danced the previous night. Johnny watched Mark, trying to read something in the big blonde's face, but could not.

Johnny threw himself into the work before him like a man possessed. The barn needed a good cleaning and that was exactly what it got. Between them, Mark and Johnny did four men's work, lifting, toting, moving bales of hay and straw, and by noon they had cleaned the barn.

By noon Jaya had finished scrubbing the house. She stood in the center of the main room and looked around her. If that did not please Johnny, she thought, nothing would please him. Perhaps she had been too friendly with Mark, she could not say, but Johnny had only himself to blame if she had. At that moment Jaya heard the sound of horse's hooves. She wondered who might be calling and, not wishing to disgrace Johnny before his neighbors, she decided to take a moment to tidy her appearance before going outside.

The sound of hooves brought Johnny and Mark's attention to the visitor, as they walked from the barn to the house to fetch Jaya and allow her to inspect and comment on their work.

"Going to need some chickens for Jaya to tend," Mark drawled, then he heard the hooves and turned.

Johnny also turned, saw the oncoming rider and felt suddenly sick to his stomach. Of all the folks he had met during his last visit to the spread, the visitor was the last he expected to see—and the last he wanted to come calling under the circumstances.

Springing from the shaggy scrub horse's bare back, the newcomer dashed forward to throw arms around Johnny's neck and crush a hot little mouth to his.

The newcomer was a girl of about five foot five. Her tawny, curly hair hung in a tangle around a pert, pretty, naïve, dirty face. She had a full, rich, magnificent body which a sleeveless, tight-fitting, man's old shirt did nothing to conceal, especially as it hung open at the neck and halfway down her round, full bust. The old, patched jeans clung to her hips like she'd been molded into them, were about knee long and her legs and feet were bare.

"Hello, Tilda-Mae," Johnny said, pushing the girl back to arm's length for her body gave off a stench of stale sweat and lack of soap which had always turned him from her.

"Johnny!" she replied. "I done saw your smoke and come a-running."

She tried to move closer, but he held her off, his hands on the greasy shoulders of her shirt.

"Won't your husband mind you coming over?" he asked.

"Naw! Never gotten married. That feller he took up and run. The boys plumb chased him down to the gully country and let holes in his side. So I'm all free and ready to marry you-all."

"*Me!*" Johnny yelped.

"Why sure. Figured it'd be fittin', us going to be neighbors 'n' all."

At that moment Tilda-Mae's eyes caught a glimpse of Mark, jerked towards him and looked him over appraisingly, hungrily.

"Who-all's this here?" she asked.

"My *amigo*, Mark Counter," Johnny answered hopefully.

"Johnny."

Jaya could not have timed her arrival at a worse moment. Five seconds later and Tilda-Mae would have been throwing herself at Mark with the same reckless abandon that characterized her association with every presentable man who came along.

Whirling from Johnny, Tilda-Mae faced Jaya, suspicion and anger glowing in her eyes.

"Who-all's she?" the girl spat out.

"That's Jaya," Johnny replied, which left a lot unexplained.

"She's your wife?"

"No—" Johnny answered, meaning to say he hoped she would be soon.

"Then she's going now!" Tilda-Mae screamed. "No dirty furrin gal's going to come here and steal my man!"

With that she hurled herself forward, fingers crooked ready to snatch at Jaya's hair. Jaya fell back a couple of paces before the fury of the other girl's rush, a look of numb shock on her face at the words.

The wildly furious mountain girl did not reach Jaya, did not even set a dirty bare foot on the porch. Johnny had been standing staring, suddenly scared at the thought of what Tilda-Mae's words must mean to Jaya. For once in his life, Johnny, who had acted fast in emergencies many times, could not think of what to do.

Springing forward, Mark caught Tilda-Mae around the waist from behind, just as she reached the edge of the porch. He clamped his left arm around her, pinning down her arms as well to her waist. Instantly she began to scream and curse, her strong little body thrashing and struggling against his, her legs thrashing and hacking back.

"Le'me go!" she screamed. "I'll scratch her eyes out! I'll yank her bald-headed! The dirty, stinking furrin calico cat! Come here and glomming onto my man!"

"Honest, Jaya!" Johnny gasped, turning to the girl as Mark dragged Tilda-Mae backwards. "I never—"

With a strangled sob, Jaya turned and ran into the house, slamming the door behind her, not even offering to listen to his explanation.

One of Tilda-Mae's heels caught Mark on the shin. Having never worn shoes, the girl's feet were hard enough to pack some power behind them. Mark grunted in pain and annoyance. Then he swung the girl up from her feet, gripping her by the hair and pants seat, hoping the material would hold out. In that manner, keeping her bucking, writhing body at arm's length, Mark carried Tilda-Mae towards the horse trough. One way or another that foul-mouthed, dirty little mountain girl needed cooling off and a bath. Mark reckoned he was the man to attend to that.

Tilda-Mae gave a scream as she hit the water and disappeared under its surface. Coming up, she started to scream curses so Mark shoved her under again. This time he held her under until he figured she ought to have learned her lesson. A gasping, sobbing, water-spitting girl sat up in the trough, but she neither struggled nor cursed. While never having received any formal schooling, Tilda-Mae knew she had best yell "calf rope" and give in, or be ducked under again.

Seeing the girl had quit struggling, Mark stepped back and allowed her to drag her soaking little body from the trough. She glared across to where Johnny stood trying to decide what to do, how to explain things to Jaya, how to stop Jaya leaving him.

"Bring that dirty furrin gal here, will you?" Tilda-Mae screamed. "Just you wait 'til my kin hears what you done, Johnny Wade. They'll fix your wagon, but good, see if they don't. Then I'll get that furrin gal and beat her so ugly she'll never steal another American gal's man."

All the time she screamed at Johnny, Tilda-Mae was backing away and keeping a wary eye on Mark. She saw the anger in his eyes as he started towards her, so spun on her heel and went atop her horse with a lithe bound. Her final threat to Jaya came as she sent the horse running up the bush-covered slope down which she came on her arrival.

Not until the sound of the horse's hooves had died away did either man make a move. Johnny let out his breath in a long, hissing sigh and turned on his heel towards the house. The only thing he could do was go in, explain things to Jaya

and hope she believed him. Before he could take three
steps, Johnny felt a hand clamp on his arm and pull him
around. He could never remember seeing Mark so angry as
the big blonde appeared to be at the moment.

"Why didn't you mention the gal?" Mark snapped.

"Why should I?" Johnny replied. "Hell, I didn't but meet
her a couple or so times last time I was up here. We had
some loving, not much, I like mine washed and not smelling like a Kiowa wickiup. You saw how she looked at you,
that gal's plumb man-hungry. Anyways, one day she came
over and told me she wouldn't be seeing me again as she
was marrying up with a traveling salesman who was working the county. I never even mentioned marrying her, and
right after that I came back to the O.D. Connected. But I
never said, or even gave Tilda-Mae cause to reckon I'd
marry her."

"Didn't, huh?"

"No, I damn well didn't!" Johnny answered, his temper
and voice rising. "What the hell is it to you? Reckon it'll
give you a better in with Jaya?"

Mark looked at Johnny for a moment. Then he made a
reply which he hoped would show his *amigo* that he (Mark)
had no designs on Jaya, and doubted if she would give a
damn even if he did have.

"I don't need a chance with Jaya," was what Mark said.

Then Johnny hit him.

Taken any way a man looked at it, except on the receiving end, Johnny could throw a good punch. His right arm
whipped around, he ducked his shoulder behind the punch
and drove his knuckles against the side of Mark's jaw. Mark
spun around and only with an effort did he manage to keep
on his feet.

Coming in, Johnny ripped his left fist into Mark's stomach and smashed up the right at Mark's jaw, for he packed
enough muscle and heft to fold Mark with the first blow.

The blow sent Mark backwards but did not put him
down. Only just in time he caught his balance and
clenched his fists for Johnny was coming at him again.

"Jaya's a good kid!" Johnny spat, closing in on Mark. "I'm
going to make sure you stay away from her."

He threw his right at Mark's head, but this time Mark

was ready. Up came Mark's left, his wrist deflecting the right past his head. Then Mark drove out his right, smashing it into Johnny's mouth and knocking him backwards. Johnny hit the dining-room table, which fortunately had been stoutly built. Instead of it crumpling under Johnny's weight, the table took it and Johnny went straight over.

"It's time you woke up!" Mark growled, coming forward. "Jaya isn't—"

With a snarl of rage, Johnny came to his feet and threw the table over in his eagerness to get at Mark. There was no avoiding a fight. Mark knew it. He also knew he would not have an easy time fighting Johnny, the cowhand was almost as big and strong as Mark and had learned many of Mark's fighting tricks during their friendship.

Mark snapped Johnny's head back with a right hand, stopping him in his tracks. Instantly Johnny's left flashed out like a diamondback rattlesnake striking. The knuckles caught Mark in the mouth and Mark felt the salty taste of blood on his soft palate. He saw how Johnny stood, perfectly balanced, his left held out maybe just a little low, but his right cocked in front of his shoulder the way Mark had taught him.

"You're learning, Johnny," Mark said.

Feinting with his right, Johnny threw another left, but Mark moved his head far enough to let the blow slip over his shoulder. Johnny brought the stiff edge of his arm against the side of Mark's neck, knocking him off balance and then slugged his left into Mark's ribs bringing a grunt of pain. Shooting out his right, Mark drove it hard into Johnny's stomach, ripped a left after it and hooked a short left viciously to the side of Johnny's jaw. The force of the blow dropped Johnny to his knees.

Even as Mark moved in, Johnny flung himself forward, tackling the big blonde around the knees and ramming him backwards. Mark felt himself going down and as Johnny lunged forward hooked his feet under the other's belly and heaved. Looking as if he had taken wings, Johnny sailed through the air to land on his back. He rolled over and came up fast, reaching his feet as soon as Mark did.

Once more Mark moved into the attack, wanting to keep Johnny away from the furniture. Sure Johnny wanted a fight, but that did not mean they should wreck his home having it.

The two men closed, fists stabbing out, ripping into each other. Mark took a savage hook to the floating ribs and went down to his knees. Up lashed Johnny's knee, driving under Mark's chin and throwing him onto his back. Johnny leapt up into the air, meaning to land on Mark with his knees. Too late he saw Mark roll, he missed but managed to break his fall. Without rising, Mark flung himself onto Johnny and they rolled over and over, fists thudding into flesh. Breaking apart, they rolled away from each other and got on their feet once more.

Driving out his fist, Mark crashed it into the side of Johnny's head and Johnny went down. Instead of attacking immediately, Mark stood back and allowed Johnny to get on his feet. They were both breathing hard, blood ran from Mark's mouth and Johnny's nose seemed to be twice its normal size. Yet Johnny still was not done. When Mark moved in, Johnny caught him with a left jab which landed under his eyes, then closed with a two-fisted, slugging attack. Mark fought back, for almost five minutes they slugged it out like that. Then Johnny twisted around, getting his arms under Mark's armpits from behind, curling them around to clamp fingers behind Mark's neck.

They were locked in a struggle of strength, Johnny applying pressure with his full nelson and Mark fighting it off. Mark tried to twist free, turn and catch Johnny in the same hold. Both his body and Johnny's arms were soaked with sweat and coated with dust, so he could not escape that way.

The pain of the hold was intense. Drawing forward his stomach, Mark suddenly jerked it back again. His rump drove into Johnny's body and Johnny lost his hold, shooting back and doubling over. Turning, Mark drove up his left, the knuckles smashing into Johnny's jaw. The force of the blow lifted Johnny to his heels and tilted him over backwards to land in a cloud of dust on the ground.

Moving forward Mark dropped astride Johnny, kneeling on him. Desperately Johnny arched his back, trying to lift and roll Mark. It appeared that Johnny was not ready to listen to reason yet. Mark cocked his fist, drawing it back, his eyes, or his good eye, for his right eye had started to swell up and close, aiming at the point of Johnny's chin.

Something crashed against Mark's head. He heard a dull clang and he pitched sideways from Johnny to land on his face. Mark lifted his head; through the spinning mists and whirling lights, he saw Jaya, a furious-faced Jaya, standing above them, holding a shovel in her hands.

"Th—thanks—h—honey!" Johnny gasped and sat up.

The shovel came around and down as Johnny reached for Mark. It clanged on Johnny's head and he landed flat on his back again.

"Keep still!" she hissed, and the concentrated fury in her voice, as much as the blow, made both men obey. "What were you fighting over, who should have me and who should take the other girl?"

Neither man made any reply. Their fight, and her intervention, had left them in no condition to make flip answers, or any other kind.

"What do you think I am, Johnny Wade?" Jaya went on, her voice throbbing with emotion. "Am I just your property? Do you think I did not know that bill of sale was worthless? I saw you were a good man in the saloon. No other man had ever bothered about me enough to get me a chair. I wanted you to win me and when you did I could have cried. I hoped you would bring me with you, that I could make you care for me, marry me. I was willing to work for you, to live or die for you. Now I find you have another woman. I hate you! I never want to see you again!"

Throwing down the shovel, Jaya turned and ran blindly towards the house. She disappeared inside, slamming the door behind her. Gasping for breath, Johnny weakly forced himself to his feet. He opened his mouth to call after Jaya, but left it too late.

"Boy, we sure loused that up."

Mark's words brought Johnny around to face him. The big blonde stood rubbing his aching head which had a sizable bump that had not been present when he rose that morning.

"You've sure put me in wrong now," Johnny growled back.

"Me?"

"Yeah, you. If you hadn't been sweet-talking Jaya all the way up here I'd've told her how I felt about her."

"The hell you would," Mark answered. "You shied away from her like a horse fresh caught on the range every damned time she tried to get close to you. So I figured to show you what you was missing."

"You sure showed me," Johnny groaned. "Of all the lousy luck. I act about as dumb as a man can get—and then that man-hungry she-cat from the hills rides in and busts everything to hell and gone. I'm going to the house. Jaya'll listen to me, let me explain."

"Not the way she feels right now," Mark drawled.

"She'll list—!" Johnny began and turned.

Mark's right fist drove out, smashing into the side of Johnny's jaw with the power of a knobhead's kick. The blow took Johnny completely by surprise, it flung him from his feet and flat onto his back. This time Johnny would not be getting up. At least not for a spell. Mark hoped he would have time to do what needed doing before Johnny did get up.

"Sorry, *amigo*," he said. "It's the only way."

Walking to the horse trough, Mark pumped water over his head, clearing the dizziness out of it. He would need a clear head if he hoped to pull Johnny and Jaya out of their tangle. After sluicing his bruised, aching body, Mark walked to the house and entered.

He heard Jaya's sobs from the bedroom and went to its door. Inside the girl stood at the bed, thrusting her clothes into the bag, but leaving the items Johnny bought her, including the hat, on the end of the bed.

"I'll take you into Brownsville if you like," he said.

"I'll walk," she replied without turning around.

"If that's the way you want it," Mark drawled. "I reckon you're doing the right thing, leaving Johnny. See the way he's been acting over you when you dressed up and danced for him, and other times. Hell, he's been acting like a man in love with a gal, instead of his old self. Just shows how deceitful he is."

No reply. The sobs had ended and Jaya no longer forced her clothes into the bag, but she did not turn.

"He's a worthless cuss at best," Mark went on. "And a

hell of a liar. Why he told me that gal used to chase him last time he was up here, but that she took out to marry some other feller, not that Johnny ever wanted to marry up with her any old way. Fact being, old Johnny reckons he never wanted to marry up at all until he met you. But like I say, he's a li—"

Swinging around, Jaya flung herself at Mark, pushing him backwards.

"Where is Johnny?" she asked.

"Knowed you wouldn't want him bothering you," Mark replied. "So I left him lying out there with a busted jaw."

"You brute!" she screamed and dashed from the room.

"Johnny boy," Mark said quietly. "If you've come around, just use your fool head for once with that gal and she's yours."

By the time Mark left the house, Jaya had reached Johnny and knelt by him, pillowing his head in her lap.

"Johnny!" she gasped. "Speak to me! I love you! I will not leave you!"

Picking up a bucket, Mark filled it with water from the horse trough. There was no use Jaya spilling her heart out to Johnny unless he happened to be able to hear and appreciate it.

"You big bullying brute!" Jaya spat as Mark came up.

He barely had time to set down the bucket before she landed on him with little fists swinging. After catching a couple of blows on the chest, Mark managed to grab the girl's arms and hold them. He twisted his body and caught a kick on the hip, then saw Johnny, behind the girl's back, raising his head and grinning.

For once it seemed Johnny had used his head around the girl.

Giving out a heart-rending groan, Johnny let his head flop back again. Jaya tore herself free from Mark's hands, forgot all about him, flung herself back to Johnny. Lifting his head and shoulders, she cradled them in her arms and kissed his battered face.

Johnny slid his arms around the girl and kissed back. For a long moment they stayed locked in each other's arms. At last they separated to catch their breath.

"Johnny," Jaya breathed. "I love you!"

"Jaya gal," he replied, "not as much as I love you."

"Yes I do!"

"We're getting married, even if I have to whup ole Mark to—"

Jaya ended the threat with a kiss, then said, "Mark never meant anything to me. Nor I to him. He acted as he did to make you jealous, so you would notice me as a woman."

For a moment Johnny did not reply. Although every muscle and fiber of his body ached, he could hardly see through his right eye and his nose felt twice its normal size, Johnny had never felt so happy in his life. Nothing else mattered except that Jaya loved him.

"Reckon old Mark did just that," he said.

Then they were locked in each other's arms once more and Johnny could hardly force himself to wait until they could find a preacher and get married. With any other girl he would not even have tried to resist.

"Where's Mark?" he asked, easing himself free from her arms.

"I don't know," Jaya replied in a tone which implied she did not care either. "Oh Johnny, you're hurt!"

"I asked for it," he grinned, getting to his feet and helping her rise, then feeling at the knot she had raised on his head with the shovel. "Don't know as how I'd want to marry a gal that handy with a shovel—unless she knew how to dance in a lil bitty grass skirt."

"You wait until our marriage night," she answered. "Then I will show *you* how the maidens really do it—where are you going?"

"To find a preacher," he grinned.

"I'll help you," she said eagerly, taking his hand.

Instead of looking for a preacher, they walked to where Mark sat on the anvil in the forge. He turned towards them and showed simulated surprise when Johnny told him of the impending marriage.

"I'd have never expected it," he grinned.

"We want you to be best man," Jaya said, squeezing Johnny's hand in a gentle warning that he had best agree.

"Sure we do," Johnny agreed wholeheartedly. "I know that's the only part you ever want to play in a wedding ceremony."

"Do I get to kiss the bride without having a fight on my hands?" Mark asked.

"That depends," Johnny grinned.

"On what?"

"How long after the wedding it is when you kiss her."

Jaya looked from one man to the other. They were the first two men who had treated her decently, cared for her and showed her respect. She almost wished she had not been so free with the shovel head when they were fighting.

A flash of light flickered up on the slope above them. Just a brief flick and then it disappeared. Mark only saw it from the corner of his eye, but his brain sent out a warning.

"Duck it!" he yelled, shoving Jaya into Johnny and staggering them to one side.

His move came only just in time. A bullet hissed down from the slope, but not from where Mark had seen the reflection of the sun on some part of a weapon. Even as the crack of the shot reached their ears, Johnny had Jaya in safety, between him and the wall of the forge.

Two more shots, from different spots, came down. One struck the top of the anvil as Mark dropped behind it, then ripped off in the vicious whine of a ricochet. The other struck the top of the forge throwing brick chips into the air.

"Wade! Johnny Wade!" yelled a voice. "You come on out here and take what's coming to you."

"Who is it?" Mark asked, looking at the wagon in front of the house and wishing either he was there with his guns, or they were here with him.

"Sounds like Big Tup," Johnny replied. "Tilda-Mae's oldest brother."

That figured, if a man knew hill folks and Mark reckoned he did. The girl had returned home with word of the affront to her person, and all her male kin took down their rifles to avenge her. Only it should be the head of the clan who did the talking.

Watching the slope, Mark had three men spotted, the three who had fired at them. One lay up just on the rim, not far from where a dried-out water-course ran up the slope. The second appeared to be denned up between a couple of rocks out on the rim to the first's right. From the flash and smoke, Mark figured the third man further to the right, down behind that big old chestnut tree. The speaker had been still further along.

"How many are there in the family?" Mark asked.

"Four boys and Tilda-Mae," Johnny replied, feeling the girl's warm body writhing at his side. "Their mammy died just after Tilda-Mae was born, pappy got killed hunting a silvertip grizzly a couple of years back."

"What do they want, Johnny?" Jaya asked.

"Nothing much, honey," he lied.

"Wade!" yelled the voice again. "Talk up. Air ye ready to do the right by our lil Tilda-Mae gal?"

"Come on down and talk it out, Tup!" Johnny called back.

"There ain't no talking out to do. You marry our lil sister, or we plant you out back of the house."

"Johnny," Jaya said, looking up at him. "Did you ever tell the girl you would marry her?"

"No, honey. Honest, I never did."

"That is all I wanted to know."

Saying that, Jaya pushed past him, wriggling free and darting across the forge. Johnny sprang forward, three bullets cut the air around him and he flattened down again. The girl ran out towards the slope and from it burst Tilda-Mae on the shaggy mountain scrub horse.

Once more Johnny came to his feet, a fourth shot came down and ripped across his shoulder, tearing through flesh, but luckily not striking bone. The wound, on top of the fight he had fought, proved too much for Johnny and he dropped to the ground.

Springing to his *amigo*'s side, Mark dragged him back into cover for another bullet sprayed dirt up between Johnny's feet. Then Mark looked to see what Jaya was doing.

Tilda-Mae had left her horse and stood before Jaya.

"Please," Jaya said. "I will leave, but you must promise not to harm Johnny or Mark."

"You're going to leave, you little furrin slut!" Tilda-Mae replied. "But not 'til I've done with you. I don't take no furrin gal's leavings."

And with that she lashed her hand around, the palm

slapping across Jaya's cheek. Jaya staggered back a few steps, caught her balance only to take another savage slap.

"Dirty furrin whore!" Tilda-Mae hissed. "Don't you have the guts to try and fight back?"

Again her palm lashed out, straight into the grip of Jaya's hands. Catching the other girl's wrist, Jaya carried it up over her head, pivoting around under the arms, then bringing her hands down. Tilda-Mae howled, her feet left the ground and she thought the world had suddenly spun around. The thud with which she landed on her back jarred the wind out of her.

Before Tilda-Mae could draw breath, she thought she had been jumped by a bobcat. Jaya sprang forward, landing on Tilda-Mae, hands lashing, clawing, tearing at hair, slapping, punching and gripping flesh. For a moment Jaya had it all her own way. Then Tilda-Mae caught her breath. The attack and throw had taken the hill girl by surprise, now that surprise was wearing off, those hard little hands, ramming, squeezing legs and sharp teeth driving it away.

Watching the girls roll over and over, Mark saw his chance. He glanced up the slope and saw the three men he had located earlier. They were all in plain sight now and yelling encouragement to their sister.

Mark was reminded of the battle at Bearcat Annie's saloon in Quiet Town, both by the wild savage way in which the girls went at it, and in the way the men up the slope stood watching. Maybe he could turn Jaya and Tilda-Mae's brawl to his advantage as Dusty Fog used the fight between the three female deputies and the saloon girls to let him get his male deputies inside the saloon and take a bunch of gunmen without firing a shot.

"You all right, Johnny?" he asked.

"I'll live!" Johnny replied weakly and thickly. "Go help Jaya afore Tilda-Mae kills her."

A glance at the girls showed Mark that Johnny's fears were, if not groundless, at least not urgent. From the way Jaya went at it, they were on their feet now, she looked like she could take care of herself. Mark had not forgotten the different ways Jaya had shown her strength, both at the store and since. She might be smaller and lighter than

Tilda-Mae, but he would not say she was weaker or less able to take care of her end in the hair-yanking brawl.

"She doesn't need help. But you stay put here, or they'll make wolf bait of you. I'll do what I can."

Turning, Mark slipped from the cover of the open-sided blacksmith's forge building and darted across the open land. At any minute he expected to feel lead either slap by him, or drive into him. Yet none came and he lit down in the comparative safety of the mouth of the water-course.

"Go at her, Tilda-Mae gal!" a voice screeched from above him.

Looking upwards, Mark saw one of the brothers, a tall, gangling youth in a torn old shirt and bib overalls. The youngster, for he seemed to be young, stood on the rim, waving his rifle over his head as he encouraged his sister.

Mark started forward, keeping in the water-course and climbing up over the rocks on its bottom. Under other conditions this would have been a suicidal route, but if the fight lasted long enough, and it showed no sign or sound of abating in fury, he might reach the top unseen by the youngster.

"Yank her bald, sister!" howled the youngster.

So engrossed had he become that he did not see the shape inching through the bushes toward him. Mark had reached the head of the slope and now crawled forward on his stomach, using every bit of cover he could find. His path brought him to a halt behind the young man and his hands reached out.

The first sign the youngster had of his danger came when a pair of hands clamped hold of his ankles and heaved. Letting out a screech like a drunk Sioux Indian, the youngster landed on his face and felt himself being hauled down off the rim. His rifle had gone as he felt the hands grip him and he twisted around, fanning his right hand towards the butt of his bowie knife. Mark took aim and hit with all his skill. His fist caught the youngster's jaw, snapped his head to one side and dropped him in a limp heap on the ground.

Moving on, keeping to what cover he could find, Mark advanced towards the second brother, knowing this one would be harder to take. He looked maybe four or five years older than the one Mark had silenced. There seemed to be a hard, mean look about him and he cradled the Henry rifle with a negligent ease that did not deceive the big Texan. Give that feller half a chance and he would come spinning around with the rifle ready for use.

Yet there was no way to move in on him from behind. A feller with his looks did not pick a place where he could be sneaked up on. He leaned against one of the rocks, a coonskin cap on his head and wearing dirty buckskins, right out in the open, clear of anything even an ant could hide behind.

Bending, Mark took up a lump of rock about the size of a baseball. Then he started forward, hoping the girls kept the hillman's attention for long enough to let him get in close.

Mark took three steps, then the man glanced back. He must have been expecting one of his brothers, for he just glanced at Mark, then turned back towards the fight—and whirled around again. The rifle started to come from his arm. Mark whipped back his arm and hurled the rock. It shot forward and caught the man on the front of his coonskin cap. From the thud, Mark knew he had put the man out of mischief, but hoped not too permanently. Without a sound, the man crumpled up and flopped to the ground.

Instantly Mark went back into cover. He thought he would be shot at, but the remaining brothers must have been too absorbed in what sounded like a humdinger of a fight to see what was happening on the rim.

This proved to be the case with the third brother. In age he seemed to fit between the first and second. Leaning his back against the chestnut's stout trunk, his rifle resting at his side, the third brother gave the girls his full attention, ignoring the possibility of an attack.

A big hand came around the tree trunk and clamped on the brother's shoulder. He let out a startled squawk, grabbed down at and missed his rifle, then shot around the trunk to catch Mark's other fist full on the side of his head. He went down as if he had been boned.

Which only left Big Tup, provided the second man had not been he. There should only be the four of them. Mark reckoned Tilda-Mae's honor would be strictly family business, so only the direct kin should be along.

"You move nice, stranger," a voice said.

Mark halted, he had been moving towards a clump of bushes where he suspected Big Tup to be hiding. The man sat in front of the bushes, his rifle on his knees, not aiming at anything in particular. In size he equaled Mark and looked like he weighed maybe ten—fifteen pounds heavier. Given that he was fresh and fit, Mark could have taken Big Tup, maybe after a hard fight. In his present condition he doubted if he could.

"Must have hill blood in you," Big Tup went on. "Didn't hurt none of the boys bad, did you?"

"Beaned the one with the Henry with a rock, maybe bust his head," Mark replied, wondering if he could get in close and jump the other before he rose.

"That'd be Lenny. Serve him right. He allows to know it all about hunting. The young 'uns all right?"

"They'll likely not feel like chewing raw beef for a couple of days."

"If you put 'em off their food, I should be thanking you," Big Tup grunted. "Set a spell and let's see how that fracas 'tween Tilda-Mae and the lil furrin gal comes out. Boys'll be tolerable riled that you made 'em miss it. Ain't seed a cat fight as good as this since Maw caught Paw with that medicine show gal one time."

Then Mark got it. The code of the hills, the code of the mountain men. Tilda-Mae brought her brothers to deal with Johnny, make him marry her, but when she went down and took Jaya on it made the matter personal between the two girls and the family would not intervene as long as nobody else did. Tilda-Mae must stand or fall alone. Mark could have saved himself some time—provided Jaya licked Tilda-Mae in the fight.

"Reckon I'd best get down and see how Johnny is," Mark said.

"You 'n' him been fussing?"

"A mite."

"That boy must be able to fight, if he stood up to a feller like you," Big Tup said soberly. "Hope Tilda-Mae licks the furrin gal, we could use some good fighting blood like that in the clan. He hurt bad?"

"Caught him a bullet in the shoulder just now."

"Land-sakes!" Big Tup grunted, coming to his feet. "Why'n't you-all say so at first. Go on down to him. I'll look to the boys, then come on down myself."

Mark did not know how far he could trust the big hillman and so watched as Big Tup, moving faster than one might have expected of a man of his size, went to examine his brothers. He showed no great concern about any of their conditions and waved Mark down the slope.

It must have been some fight if the girls' appearance was anything to go by. Tilda-Mae had lost her shirt and her face carried marks. Jaya had come off better in the matter of clothes. Her skirt was torn from hem to hip and trailing behind her, her long hair in a dirty tangle, her face bruised and bloody.

Even as the men reached the foot of the slope, Tilda-Mae fell against the corral rails, hung there and reeled forward. Jaya braced herself and kicked up. While visiting New Orleans, Mark had seen French *savate* fighters and was reminded of them in the way Jaya kicked, except that they wore shoes and used the toe while Jaya's feet were bare and she kicked with the ball of her foot. The result was just as effective. Caught in the pit of the stomach, Tilda-Mae gave a scream and dropped to her knees. She landed on Jaya's other knee as the little girl leapt forward and brought it up. Coming erect again, Tilda-Mae went backwards, hit the corral rail and hung there, then her knees buckled up and she crashed forward onto her face. Reeling forward, Jaya fell against the corral fence and held herself up on it.

With no more concern than he showed when looking at his brothers, Big Tup walked forward, bent and dug his hand into Tilda-Mae's hair. He lifted the girl's head from the ground, looking at the dirty, bruised features and glazed unseeing eyes. Releasing Tilda-Mae, he let her flop to the ground once more and turned to look at Jaya who supported herself by the corral rail, gasping for breath, sobbing and trying to hold the ripped top of her dress together.

"You whupped her fair 'n' square, lil furrin gal," Big Tup said. "She won't bother you or your man again."

Bending, he lifted his sister and carried her to her horse, draping her face down over its back.

At the same moment Johnny came up, limping and with his wounded arm hanging limply at his side. In his good hand, he held a Colt.

"Let it lie, Johnny!" Mark snapped, stepping into his line of fire.

"Look at what she did to Jaya!" Johnny growled, turning his eyes to the little girl who had sunk to her knees.

"You should see what Jaya did to her," Mark grinned. "Boy, when you're all married off to her, you do what she says. That gal fights like Dusty, uses a lot of the same tricks."

At another time Johnny might have been interested to know of somebody who could use the fighting techniques so ably practiced by Dusty Fog. Right now his only interest was Jaya.

Dropping the Colt, Johnny sprang to the girl's side. She turned her face to his.

"I—I would have gone away—rather than let them hurt you," she said.

With his good arm, Johnny lifted the girl to her feet and supported her as he headed her for the house. Mark turned to watch Big Tup leading the scrub horse and its burden up the hill and saw two of the brothers on their feet. The youngest turned and jumped to where his rifle lay, but Big Tup bellowed and waved a hand at Tilda-Mae. Lowering the rifle without lining it, the young man moved down to meet Big Tup and his sister.

Picking up the Colt Johnny had dropped, Mark looked at it, then turned.

"Hey, Johnny!" he called. "The next time you decide to throw a gun around in the dirt—do it with one of your own."

Mark looked at the other two occupants of the room and grinned as he sank stiffly into a chair at the breakfast table.

"What's so funny?" Johnny growled, limping up and taking his seat.

"I was thinking what a sorry-looking bunch we look," Mark explained.

Hobbling stiffly around with the food and coffee, Jaya looked at the two men's faces and smiled.

"Do I look like you?" she asked.

"Worse," Mark replied.

It was the morning after the day of the fights. Although none of the three meant to, they had slept in late and Jaya, first awake, now served them their food. On taking her seat, she looked at Johnny and Mark, then started to giggle. Her merriment started Johnny chuckling, for he too now saw what amused Mark.

After the departure of the hill family, Mark helped Johnny to care for Jaya, then patched his *amigo*'s wound up, using a basic knowledge of such matters gained in years of hectic life. The wound proved to be more messy and painful than dangerous, but Mark put Johnny's arm in a sling to prevent him using it too much.

With Jaya and Johnny's help, and his own terrific strength, Mark unloaded the supplies and stored them in the root cellar under the house. Then he moved as much of the furniture back into the house as he could manage. After that Mark was only too willing to go to sleep.

Jaya had bathed the previous night, combed the tangles out of her hair and now, with a couple of additions, looked her usual self.

"Where'd you learn to fight like you did?" Johnny asked her. "I never saw anybody but a French-Creole kick like you did."

"It is an old Siamese fighting trick," she replied. "I was a wild child and learned to defend myself from the native children."

"You sure did," Mark grinned. "If you hadn't tangled with her, we'd likely still be out there, or dead."

"They would have killed us all?" she gasped.

"They're hill folk, mountain men. Don't go by the same standards as other people. They've lived to that code ever since their kind moved in from the East. Cut one hill feller and all his kin bleed. They live by the rules their fathers and grandfathers laid down for them. That's why they didn't shoot after you and the gal tangled. She'd made the fight a personal thing and they couldn't cut in."

"Then she won't come here again?" Jaya asked.

"Not after Johnny," Mark replied. "That's for sure. Under the code of the mountain folk she was whipped fair and square and she's got no claim on him."

"She never had," Johnny growled.

"I feel a little sorry for her," Jaya put in, ignoring Johnny's comment.

At that moment they heard hooves outside and the snort of a horse, then a voice called, "Hello, the house!"

"Tilda-Mae!" Johnny snapped, thrusting back his chair.

The girl sat her horse in front of the house. Although she wore a shirt it was not clean and she had made a very poor job of cleaning the results of the fight from her face and those parts of her body which showed; nor had she done anything about her dirty, tangled mop of hair.

"Can I see the furr—your woman, Johnny?" she asked without dismounting.

"No you c—"

Before Johnny could finish his denial, Jaya came from the house and pushed between him and Mark, stepping from the porch.

Tilda-Mae squinted down at Jaya, then looked at the two men. "Can we make women talk?"

"Of course. Get off your horse. Come in and have some breakfast. We only just rose."

Slipping from her horse, Tilda-Mae stood by it. She raised her right foot against her calf, looking embarrassed. She made no attempt to walk towards the house and Jaya turned to tell the two men to go inside.

"It's all right, Johnny," she said when he showed signs of hesitation. "Go in, please."

Once left alone words rushed out of Tilda-Mae's mouth.

"I want you to help me! I want to know why it is I can't never get a man who'll stick to me. And I don't mean Johnny. Sure I went after him, but he never said he'd marry me. But I want to know why I can't get a man."

"How would I know?" Jaya smiled.

"You furrin gals know about things like that."

Looking at the other girl, Jaya felt pity for her. Tilda-Mae was lonely and needed affection. Her brothers were kind enough in their own ways, but they did not give the girl the love and affection she craved. So she had tried to find it with other men, and never with happy results.

"I'll help you," Jaya promised, looking the other girl over. "The first thing we do is get you a bath—"

"A *bath!*" Tilda-Mae gasped. "You mean all over, without any clothes on?"

"Of course. A man likes a girl to smell nice. Come, I found some clothes belonging to Johnny's aunt, they might fit you, and there are other things that we can use."

"Yeah, but—" Tilda-Mae groaned, hanging back at the awful thought of having a bath.

"It's the only way," Jaya warned, taking Tilda-Mae's grubby little hand and leading her gently towards the house.

Neither Johnny nor Mark knew what Jaya planned. She gave them orders to go out and find some work, but not to come in until she called for them.

At noon, still with no sign of the two girls, Johnny saw something which took his mind temporarily off thoughts of what Tilda-Mae might be doing to his Jaya.

A large party of people were coming towards the house. Four buggies carrying neighboring families rolled in the center of some twenty or more men. In the lead of the party, spurring his horse forward, rode Big Tup.

"Howdy, Johnny," he greeted, sliding the horse to a halt. "Real sorry about your arm. That big feller near on cracked Lenny's head and raised lumps on Sam and Jeb. Reckon we can call it evens?"

"If that's the way you want it," Johnny replied, throwing a puzzled look at the approaching party.

"Preacher's in town," Big Tup remarked. "So I sent the boys out to gather in your neighbors. Figured you and the fu—your gal'd like company on the way in to see him."

By that time the others of the party had arrived and broad grins came to every face as they studied Johnny.

"Where-at's your gal, Johnny?" asked a stout woman. "We didn't know you'd got here or we'd've come over to lend a hand."

"Jaya!" Johnny called.

The house door opened and Jaya came out. There were mutters of admiration and surprise at her appearance, but what the crowd saw following her really made them sit back and stare.

"Is that you, Tilda-Mae?" Big Tup gasped.

His surprise had good cause. The girl behind Jaya was clean, her hair still curly but soft looking and tidy, and she wore a gingham dress of modest pattern. During the morning Jaya had searched through the drawers of the side-piece and found clothes belonging to Johnny's dead aunt; she died some eighteen months before his uncle. For the first time in her life Tilda-Mae wore clean underclothes instead of old flour-sack drawers and she liked the feeling. She also liked the admiring looks several young men threw her way, but remembered Jaya's advice about not throwing herself at men so stood demure and unspeaking.

"Jaya," Johnny said. "There's a preacher down at Bagley's Corners. Do we want to see him?"

"Yes, Johnny," she gasped. "Yes, please!"

And she threw her arms around his neck, kissing him, then moved away with a blush on her cheeks as the watching people laughed. Her embarrassment did not last for the women of the party bore down on her, sweeping her and Tilda-Mae back into the house to do the things women must always do before a wedding.

It made a pretty picture. The bride standing blushing shyly at the side of the very nervous groom. The best man and bridesmaid in their places, the guests seated on cracker boxes, chairs and the bench brought in from its usual place on the store's porch. Bagley's Corners had not yet grown in size to the point where a preacher could live as a permanent thing, or to where a church became a necessity.

Standing with his back to the assembled crowd, the preacher prepared to start the ceremony. When the rustling and shuffling died away behind him, he turned to face the congregation.

First he looked at Jaya's puffed and swollen left eye and scratched cheek. Next his eyes went to Johnny's swollen nose and almost-closed right eye. From there his gaze took in Tilda-Mae who sported two blackened eyes and a lump on her forehead and Mark whose left eye matched Johnny's right and whose top lip looked twice its normal size. After that the preacher looked at the crowd, to Tilda-Mae's three brothers who each bore signs of how the big blond Texan handled them; and finally to a pair of young men who carried more recent signs of a discussion as to who should escort this new, clean Tilda-Mae to town.

After traveling the Texas range for nearly twenty years in a vain attempt to save unruly souls, the preacher reckoned he could not be surprised anymore. If the sight before him had not been a surprise, it would do until one came along. However, he rallied quickly.

"Dearly beloved," he said. "It sure looks like you had a hard time convincing each other it was time to come to church."

For a moment Jaya and Mark's eyes met and the girl smiled.

"We did," she breathed. "But we made it in the end."

3

THE KIDNAPPERS

A sudden crash! The batwing doors of the Indian Nations Saloon burst open and the citizens of Guthrie, Oklahoma Territory—or such of them as chanced to be in the vicinity at that moment—were treated to the spectacle of Fatso Kinnear erupting into the street. He came out all doubled over, like a man who had been kicked in the belly by a mule, or hit there by a real powerful fist. On the street he dropped to the hoof-churned dirt and lay writhing in agony upon it.

An instant after Kinnear's arrival on the street, the batwing doors flew open once more and his partner, Lou Rushton, came into sight running backwards, or so it seemed. At least his stubby fat legs moved as if running, although they continued to do so after he left the sidewalk. Then he lit down on his feet and flopped backwards to crash down across Kinnear's bloated form.

Again the doors opened, although with less violence, as Mark Counter and his cousin Beau emerged. They halted on the sidewalk and looked down at the recumbent forms of their attackers with dispassionate gaze.

"It looks like they're plumb tuckered out, Cousin Mark," said Beau, calmly setting right his gray cutaway jacket, for he was a professional gambler and always liked to appear neatly dressed when his funds ran to it.

"Looks that way, Cousin Beau," Mark agreed. "I take it you'd won some and they didn't like losing."

"Amazing deduction. They sat in the game half an hour back and I warned them I intended to pull out at ten o'clock. But when the time came they objected to my going."

Beau's accents sounded different than Mark's deep south drawl for he had spent several years in England and picked up the speech of the upper-class folks he mingled with.

"If they'd known you, they'd've been pleased to see you go," grinned Mark. "It might have given them a chance to win."

"My dear old cousin, that pair couldn't count to eleven without taking off their shoes—I won't say socks, they probably don't wear any. Come along the street a piece, I've something for you."

A few people had gathered around, looking at the groaning shapes on the ground. One of the crowd wore the badge of a deputy town marshal, but he made no attempt to stop Mark and Beau as they walked away. Bounty hunters had never been held in respect by lawmen of the better kind. Kinnear and Rushton were even viler than most of their breed. The deputy knew they had come into Guthrie the previous day bringing in three dead outlaws, two of whom had been shot in the back, to make collection on the bounty their heads carried.

Being unmoved by public disapproval, Kinnear and Rushton took their blood money to the Indian Nations Saloon and found a big stake poker game in progress. They sat in and found Beau among the players. Not being skillful poker players, their money soon faded away, most of it going in the mistaken belief that Rushton could fill an inside straight on the draw.

Which was when the trouble started. Beau had already announced his time for quitting the game, both knew of his decision. Yet when the appointed hour arrived they raised violent objections to his going. Their objections brought Mark into the affair for his cousin faced odds of two to one in numbers and almost three to one in weight.

Actually Beau could probably have managed the two men single-handed. Mark definitely could, for neither Rushton nor Kinnear had the courage of cornered rats when put to the test. However, Mark cut in and rendered Kinnear incapable of enjoying his food for some time to come, while Beau demonstrated his fistic prowess on the no more able Rushton.

Seeing the local law did not appear to have the intention of taking their part, Rushton dragged himself to his feet. He wore an Army Colt at his side but did not touch it. Not that his scruples would have prevented him shooting a man in the back, but he knew the deputy would intervene should he try.

Helping the moaning Kinnear to his feet, Rushton half dragged, half carried him from the street.

At the hotel Mark and Beau prepared to go their separate ways. Beau intended to catch a stage and Mark wished to collect his horse and head down trail on his business.

"About that thousand you lent me to sit in the game, old son," Beau said, taking out his wallet. "I rather improved on it. Here."

Mark accepted the sheaf of hundred dollar bills and riffled them through his fingers.

"Feels like there's more than a thousand here," he remarked.

"Two actually. Call the other interest on your loan."

"You don't need to pay me interest, Cousin Beau."

"I know. But take it anyway," Beau replied. "I'm always luckier if I show a bit of generosity, and I couldn't have got into the game without your help. So put it away and don't argue. I'd force it on you, only I'd get licked."

Grinning at his cousin, Mark put the money into his own wallet and slid the wallet under his shirt to the special pocket built inside.

"I don't feel like licking anybody today," he said.

"Where are Dusty and the Kid?" Beau asked.

"They headed straight down to the O.D. Connected. What with the delay we had on the way up, with that trouble on the Lindon Land Grant,* and running the law

---

* Told in *Trigger Fast* by J. T. Edson.

in Mulrooney, they wanted to get back fast. But I heard
Pappy was bringing a herd up the west trail and came this
way to see him."

"If I was staying in town for the night we could whoop
things up a bit. I know a couple of young ladies who're just
pining for the company of a brace of fine, fit and frolicsome
Southern gentlemen. But I've booked a passage on the
northbound stage and there's a big game I want to catch
due to start in Mulrooney so I can't cancel it."

"Sure," Mark drawled. "I want to be riding myself. See
you, Cousin Beau."

"Sure, Cousin Mark. Don't take any wooden women."

"I leave that to your side of the family. *Adios.*"

With that Mark turned and headed for the livery barn
where his horse waited for his pleasure. Beau entered the
hotel to collect his belongings. Neither noticed the two
girls who had followed them along the street, listening to
every word they said.

Riding his seventeen-hand stallion at an easy trot along
the winding trail from Guthrie, Mark made for the western
slope of the cattle drives which came up from Texas. Some-
where on the western trail he would meet his father's herd,
visit for a spell, then head back to the O.D. Connected.

The noose of rope came flying from the side of the trail,
sent out in a hooley-ann throw to drop over Mark's head
and around his shoulders, then draw tight. Although taken
by surprise, Mark did not panic. Allowing the reins to fall,
he stopped his horse. His right leg kicked free of the stir-
rup, over the saddlehorn and he dropped to the ground.
With a sudden heave of his enormous biceps, he opened his
arms. The rope jerked and he heard a startled feminine
yelp, then a thud as the one who roped him shot out of the
bushes. Mark started to turn, the rope still on him and
slowing his move towards his guns.

A bullet kicked up dirt between his feet. The shot, a flat
bark of a Winchester carbine, came from the opposite side
to where the rope came.

"Just freeze solid, big boy!" warned an unmasculine
voice.

Keeping his hands still, Mark turned towards the

speaker. She stood at the side of the trail, having stepped from concealment. Working the lever of her carbine, she kept Mark covered.

The girl wore a white Stetson on the back of a mop of close cut, curly black hair. She was a good-looking girl, probably not more than eighteen years old at most, with her skin tanned by much time spent in the open. The tartan shirt she wore, and the jeans with their turned-back cuffs, emphasized a slim, but not bony build. She wore high-heeled cowhand boots, and a gunbelt, with a Navy Colt in its holster at her right side, hung around her waist.

Just as slowly, Mark turned to look at his captor. She stood in the trail where his sudden jerk had heaved her, the rope still gripped in her hands. In height she came maybe to her pard's shoulder, but did not have a slim build. Rather there was a rubbery plumpness about her, not fat, but the kind of build which allowed its owner to be as agile as many a slimmer person. Her hairstyle copied her friend's, was mousybrown, and if anything more curly. Her face bore a warm, vibrant, merry, if naïve charm. Mark put her age at maybe a year less than the other girl's. A black Stetson hung by its storm strap onto her back. The blue shirt fitted tightly to her body, and the jeans looked stretched almost to their limits. At her left side, the holster and gun looking like mates to the one her friend wore, hung a Navy Colt. Her face showed amazement at having been plucked out of her hiding place with no more effort than if she had been a feather.

"Haul that rope tight again, Britches!" the slim girl ordered. "One wrong move'll see you limping, big boy."

"Annie could do it, too, mister," warned the chubby girl, her voice a little high with excitement.

The chance dropped names, if it had been by chance, puzzled Mark. Sure he had heard of Cattle Annie and Little Britches, but he always discounted them as being no more than camp followers of the Doolin gang. Messengers or lookouts kept around to amuse the male members with their pose of being desperate lady outlaws.

Having met Doolin on two occasions, not connected with the outlaw's professional life, Mark liked the man. It did not fit in with Mark's ideas of Doolin's character that the outlaw would allow Cattle Annie and Little Britches to do the dirty and risky work of holdup while he and the other men stayed hidden. In fact it seemed highly unlikely that Doolin would waste time robbing chance-passing strangers. Finally, apart from their friendship, Doolin would not risk antagonizing a man as dangerous as Mark Counter; a man with capable, tough and good friends to back him, or take the vengeance trail should Mark be shot in a robbery.

He allowed the rope to tighten, for Cattle Annie held the carbine like she knew how to use it. Remembering Doolin boasting about the girl's sighting eye, Mark knew better than to object.

"Now ease your hands round in front of you," Annie ordered and Mark obeyed.

Showing skill in the handling, Little Britches sent two coils of rope flipping out to settle around his arms and draw tight. Now Mark remained very still. Given a chance and a few minutes to work up to it, he might have snapped the three strands of hard-plaited Manila rope around him, but not in time to stop the girl in front planting lead into him.

"Cover him, Britches!" Annie ordered, leaning her carbine against a bush. "And keep that rope tight."

Stepping forward, Annie lugged a pair of old Bean Giant handcuffs from her hip pocket. Mark tensed himself, but felt something hard and round gouge into his back. Something about right for the size of the business end of a Navy Colt. Doolin allowed Britches to be fair with a carbine and handy with a light-caliber Colt. Even if she could not shoot like Dusty Fog, the girl would be highly unlikely to miss at that range, and Mark had heard her cock the Colt as she approached.

Had there been men along Mark could have acted in a different manner. A man could not kick a girl in the guts, then jump her to get a weapon, which he might have chanced with a man. He knew Doolin would soon put an end to such foolishness. Which worried Mark. Where was Doolin?

The handcuffs clicked onto his wrists. They looked like an old pair, probably stolen from some sheriff's office. He hoped the girls had a key, although it did not worry him a great deal if they had not.

"Don't tickle," he warned as Annie bent to unlash the support thongs on the bottom of his holsters.

Yet Mark felt puzzled. He could not see why the girls would take the trouble to handcuff him if robbery was their plan. Nor would they waste time in taking off his gunbelt.

Slinging Mark's gunbelt around her shoulders, Annie stepped back. Britches removed the rope with the easy speed of a cowhand and stood grinning at the other girl.

"It worked, Annie," she said. "Just like we planned it."

"Sure," Annie replied, turning to walk towards Mark's horse.

"Watch him, gal!" Mark ordered. "He doesn't take to strangers handling him."

To prove its master's words the big stallion swung its head towards the girl, snorting a warning. Annie showed she knew something about horses. Talking quietly and steadily, she walked towards the horse. Out shot her hand to haul the rifle from the saddlebag, then she sprang clear and avoided a vicious chop from the stallion's jaws.

"What now?" Mark asked, puzzled at the girls' actions.

"You're coming with us," Britches replied, stepping around him, having holstered her Colt while she coiled the rope.

"Why?" Mark asked.

"Why'd you think?" Annie answered.

Mark did not reply in words, but his smile brought an angry flush to Annie's face and caused Britches to giggle.

"Not for *that!*" Annie snorted.

"You wouldn't need to hawg-tie me if it was," grinned Mark. "Why then?"

"We know you, Mark Counter. Your pappy's coming up trail right now."

"So?"

"So we figure he'll pay a thousand dollars to get you back," Britches explained and Annie frowned at her for stealing the thunder.

It took Mark almost thirty seconds to get what Britches meant.

"How long's Bill Doolin gone in for kidnapping?" he asked.

"Shucks, this isn't Bill's idea," Britches replied. "It's mine —well, mine and Annie's."

Her amendment came as she saw a frown crease Annie's brow.

"Sure," Annie agreed. "Bill and the boys went out to pull off a raid and left us at a hideout. Only we come into Guthrie, saw you, learned who you was and where you was headed. Came out here, laid in wait and caught you. Ole Bill doesn't know spit about this."

That figured, if a man came to think about it. Bill Doolin must be far away for the girls to be trying such foolishness. Mark knew Doolin would put an end to the farce quickly enough should he return. So Mark reckoned he might as well go along with the girls. His father's herd would not be close enough for them to deliver the ransom message for several days and by that time anything could have happened to set Mark free.

"On your hoss, big boy," Annie ordered. "And no tricks, or they'll be calling you Limpy."

While Mark swung afork his horse, Annie threw a bullet into his rifle's chamber. Britches hurried off to return with a pair of wiry ponies. She mounted one, jerking the carbine from its saddlebag, after strapping on her rope to the horn. Annie stowed her carbine and retained Mark's rifle in her hands to help keep the big Texan under control.

"Get going, and don't try a trick," Britches ordered.

"Nary a trick, ma'am," replied Mark, now thoroughly enjoying the unusual experience of being kidnapped by a pair of pretty little girls. "Where'd you want for me to go?"

"Turn right into the trees," Annie replied. "We'll point you from there."

They rode for a time in silence, Mark in the lead and the two girls like the twin points of the letter V behind him. However as they left the wooded land behind them and wound through the rolling Indian Nations land, Britches could restrain herself no longer.

"Boy!" she said, bringing her pony alongside Mark's stallion. "Won't this shake ole Bill down to his toes. And Red

Buck and the rest. We'll make a thousand on our first chore."

"Sure," Annie agreed delightedly. "And they wouldn't take us with 'em this time in case the going got rough. I bet they take us along in future."

Mark considered this highly likely, or that Doolin would throw them out on their rumps for pulling such a fool trick. He could imagine Doolin's comments when the outlaw heard the two girls had been stupid enough to think of kidnapping Mark Counter and asking for a ransom from his father, Big Rance Counter. Mark also thought that the girls might find Doolin's reaction far from the one they hoped to receive.

For a pair of bold, daring kidnappers, the girls made a bad mistake. They took trouble to hide their tracks and stuck to country over which the following of signs would be a slow, difficult proceeding. Yet they made no attempt to blindfold him and prevent him seeing where they took him.

After covering some five miles from the trail, the girls pointed Mark down into a wide, winding valley. The slopes rose fairly steep, with a scattering of rocks, trees and bushes covering them, but the bottom lay open and offered good grazing.

Turning a bend in the valley brought them into sight of a small log cabin. A snug retreat well hidden from prying eyes. To one side of it lay a spring which widened into a deep pool and trickled off in a stream which ran through the edges of a couple of pole corrals. Although the corrals had no horses in them, they had been in recent use. All in all the place looked ideal for gentlemen following Mr. William Doolin's self-effacing business.

"Get yourself down, big boy," Annie ordered as they reached the corrals. "Watch him, Britches, while I tend to the hosses."

"You-all reckon you can handle that big blood bay of mine, Annie-gal?" asked Mark, swinging from his saddle.

Annie bit her lip, eyeing the stallion doubtfully. This was a snag she and Britches had not foreseen when they rode into Guthrie meaning to find somebody to rob as proof for Doolin for their capabilities. Of course, they had not thought of kidnapping anybody, either. The idea came to them after they left town meaning to merely hold Mark up and empty his wallet. Then Annie had her brilliant idea, to pull off a more impressive and better-paying job. Now she found a problem, for her love of horses would not allow her to neglect the big stallion. Yet she could see no way out of the predicament.

"If I give my word will you unlock one cuff and let me tend to him?" Mark suggested.

For a moment Annie did not reply. She looked Mark over from head to foot, then glanced at Britches, seeking advice.

"You'll give us your solemn word not to try anything and let us fasten you soon as you're done?" Britches asked.

"As solemn as they come, and they don't come solemner," Mark replied, hoping the amusement he felt did not show.

The two girls drew away and went into a huddle, talking and throwing looks in his direction. Mark watched them, leaning against the corral rail and awaiting their decision.

"Don't you try nothing," Annie warned, taking the handcuffs key from her pants pockets.

"Ma'am!" Mark answered, drawing himself up indignantly, "if you're doubting a Southern gentleman's word—"

"Shuckens, no!" Britches put in. "We wouldn't do that."

Clearly the two girls accepted that he would keep his word, for Annie unlocked the handcuffs without taking any precautions such as handing either Mark's gunbelt which hung around her shoulders, or her own revolver, to Britches. If Mark had wished, he could have drawn the nearest of his Colts and disarmed the girls. He did not. After all, a man ought to keep his solemn given word to a pair of gallant lady outlaws.

After attending to his horse, Mark carried his saddle to the lean-to behind the house and hung it alongside the girls' on the burro. Then, as solemnly as Lee offering his sword to Grant at the Appomattox Courthouse, he held out his right arm and allowed Annie to secure it.

"March to the house," Annie ordered.

Grinning, Mark marched. His horse stood in one corral,

the girls' mounts in the other. Annie brought her carbine and Mark's rifle along and Britches carried her carbine under her arm.

The door opened into the main room of the cabin, with a stove and cooking range to one side, a rough table and maybe half a dozen chairs as the sole furnishings. A wall split the cabin in two parts, the rear being given over to a couple of bedrooms.

Britches saw the way Mark looked around him and her cheeks flushed a little.

"This's just a layoff place," she said. "You should oughta see our main hideout, it's got rugs on the floor, even a pianny. Ain't that so, Annie?"

"It sure enough is," Annie agreed. "Make yourself to home, mister. We'll fix you a meal, then you can write us a note to deliver to your pappy, telling him what we aim to do to you if he don't pay up."

She hung Mark's gunbelt on a peg by the door, and put the rifle and carbine on the racks which lined the walls. A happy smile came to Cattle Annie's face. It sure would be great to show Bill and the boys that they could handle their share of the business.

For almost an hour Fatso Kinnear had been cursing the man who laid him low after rough-handling him. While it never was much to look at, his fat face had an ashy greenish shade which made it even more repulsive.

His partner did not say much, though less from a spirit of Christian forgiving of his enemies than because his swollen jaw did not make for easy talking. So he stood scratching his long, shaggy hair and thinking on much the same lines as Kinnear spoke.

The two bounty hunters stood in the cheap livery stable which doubled as a place to leave their horses and a hotel room for themselves. True Guthrie was a fair-sized city with several hotels and rooming houses, but every one appeared to be booked up solid when the two bounty hunters arrived asking for a place to sleep while in town. On hearing of their problem, the owner of the livery barn generously offered to allow them to sleep in an empty stall mostly used for penning his pigs.

"How about the smell?" Rushton had asked when presented with the magnanimous offer.

"Don't worry," the owner replied. "The pigs won't mind it."

Rushton still did not know how to take the remark.

"I'll kill that big blond feller, see if I don't!" Kinnear snarled, showing a remarkable lack in inventive powers as he had made the threat at least six times. "You see if I don't."

At that moment the third member of their evil organization entered the barn and slouched towards the two men. He came silently, for he wore Indian moccasins. Nor did the Indian motif end there. His fringed buckskins smelled like a Kiowa lodge and had been greased and smoke-blackened to a pitch where they could be located when downwind—and upwind too, if a man had a delicate nose. His face bore the high cheekbones, the slightly hooked nose and slit-eyed look of an Indian, yet had a sickly pallor. Sunset Charlie Mallalieu's mother had been an Osage Indian who even the Osages regarded as being beyond the pale; his father, a white of French birth, although he always celebrated a festival called Yom Kippur. The half-breed inherited the worst characteristics of both races and none of their good points.

"I found-um something," he said, hitching up his gunbelt, with its Beals Navy revolver at the right and bowie knife at the left side.

"Who?" asked Kinnear.

"Those two gals who ride wit' Doolin. I found out who they is from Injun feller. Him say they gals who ride with Doolin all right."

"Got mon' on 'em?" mumbled Rushton.

By this he did not ask if the girls carried money on their persons, but if any interested law-enforcement body had offered a reward for their capture dead or alive, preferably the first.

"No. them gals not impo't' enough," Mallalieu replied.

"Then why in hell are you coming bothering us?" demanded Kinnear; his stomach seemed to be trying to crawl up his throat as he caught a whiff of the half-breed's stench.

"Them leave town. I see-um go. Maybe-so they go to Doolin's hideout."

Instantly the other two sat up and took notice. Bill Doolin and his bunch carried big money on their heads. Higher than Kinnear and Co. had ever made, for they tended to be coyotes rather than buffalo wolves in their line. If their financial situation had been better they might have passed up going after the Doolin gang as far too risky. But, as Kinnear and Rushton were all too painfully aware, beggars could not be choosers.

"Word has-um that Doolin and his boys away on raid," Mallalieu went on. "Maybe them gals lead us to-um straggler."

"Yeah," muttered Rushton. "They could at that. Let's go see."

They took their horses and belongings, slipped out of town and Mallalieu pointed out the girls' tracks. At first the half-breed found no difficulty in following the trail of the two horses. He led the way to where they left their horses among the trees and read the story left by their feet. It appeared that the girls had set up a holdup on the trail, although none of the trio could think why, nor could they decide why the man the girls stopped should accompany them into the trees.

"Looks like they met up with the feller to take him back to their hideout," Kinnear remarked.

"Let's take after him," Rushton replied, speaking with difficulty.

However, tracking the three horses became more difficult once they left the trees behind. Although Mallalieu could cling to the trail, it took good and careful sign-reading to do so, and good and careful sign-reading could not be done at a gallop. Their slow rate of progress did nothing to improve Kinnear's and Rushton's tempers, for it prevented them from getting close enough to even see their prospective victims. Had they done so their plan of action would have been simple yet effective: sneak up when the three riders were bedded down for the night and pour a volley of rifle fire from the darkness into the sleeping camp.

"No see-um tracks any more," Mallalieu announced.

"Leave it until daylight then," Kinnear answered. "We'll camp here and move on at dawn."

The first light of dawn found them with a problem. Rushton's jaw was so swollen that he could barely speak a coherent word. Yet he did not trust the other two enough to allow them to go on without him. They rode on and came to a wide valley with steep slopes covered with rocks, bushes and trees. Here Mallalieu drew his horse to a halt and cocked his head to one side, listening.

"They close," he said.

Kinnear swung from his saddle and drew the rifle from the boot. He saw the other two had followed his lead and nodded his head.

"Let's move in and take a look," he said.

Give them their due, Cattle Annie and Little Britches might be no more than a couple of fool kids playing at being outlaws, but they sure could whomp up a mess of hog jowls and mustard greens fit to set before a king.

Mark ate well, despite the handicap of being handcuffed and having his ankles roped together in an effective hobble which would not permit him to walk at anything faster than a snail's pace. In payment for his meal Mark entertained the girls with jokes and stories, keeping them laughing and making a favorable impression on them both. He noticed the way Britches studied his great spread of shoulders and slim waist with interest. And, although she tried to hide it, Annie was taking in his handsome features, noticing the virile, vital health of his giant physique. This did not surprise Mark, for he was used to attracting the interested looks of females.

With the supper done, Mark suggested he help Britches wash the dishes. He sensed rather than saw Annie watching them. The elder girl grunted her disapproval as Mark, seemingly by accident, bumped into Britches who began to giggle. When the dishes were done Annie told Britches to watch the big feller and walked from the cabin.

"Ain't she the bossy one though?" grinned Mark.

"Yeah!" agreed Britches. "Ain't she?"

Only she did not grin and there was a hint of annoyance

in her eyes. They said no more until the other girl entered and spread Mark's bedroll on the floor by the wall.

"You sleep there, big boy," she ordered. "I'll stand the first night herd on him, Britches."

"Reckon we need to?" Britches replied suspiciously.

"Sure we need to. We'll look real fools if he sneaks off in the night."

For a moment the desire to go to bed and suspicion of Annie's motives warred on Britches's pretty little face. Then she turned and headed for the bedroom door, turning towards Annie as she reached it.

"Mind you call me for my watch!" she warned. "I'll leave the door open in case *you* need help."

An angry frown creased Annie's face as she watched Britches's fat little rump disappear into the bedroom, but she did not reply. Instead she began to tidy up the cabin, while Mark remained seated at the table. After finishing her tidying, Annie took the two carbines and cleaned them. By the time she had finished, the bubbling snores coming from the bedroom told her Little Britches was asleep.

"She snores worse'n a hawg at times," Annie remarked, bringing the coffeepot from the stove. "Are you all right?"

"I've been more comfortable."

"Shuckens, you can lie down if you like."

"The night's young. I'd rather sit and talk."

"Always say a man talks better with a coffee cup in his hands," she replied. "What do you want to talk about?"

"Weather, if you like."

"Whether I will, or whether I won't?" snapped Annie.

"The thought had crossed my mind," grinned Mark. "What'd be the answer?"

"That depends on who asked."

"Me, I'm asking."

"Bill and the boys'll be back by nighttime tomorrow, if everything goes smooth," Annie said, speaking rapidly as she changed the subject. "Won't they be surprised when they find you here?"

Surprised was not the word Mark would have used.

"How come you two get tied in with Bill and his bunch?" he asked.

It all began when the Doolin gang paid a courtesy call to the small village where Cattle Annie and Little Britches lived, the girl explained. The outlaws came to attend a wedding and dance. They intrigued the local kids and made themselves pleasant to the citizens for Doolin knew the value of good public relations even though he had never heard of them.

To the youngsters of the area Doolin's gang carried an aura of glamour. But Annie McDougall and Jennie Stevens did more than just sit back and watch from afar. When Doolin's gang rode out of the town, the two girls took their horses and borrowed men's clothing and followed. Once Doolin chased them back, but they tagged along and showed up at his hideout. After that Doolin could hardly risk allowing them to go back.

So they became Cattle Annie and, from the way she filled her pants, Little Britches. They were accepted as the mascots of the gang, for Doolin's bunch had a string of good fortune starting from their arrival. The outlaws treated them with kindness, protected them, and taught them a number of things girls from honest, God-fearing homes only rarely learned about; such as how to handle a rifle or a revolver and how to take care of themselves by using their fists instead of hair yanking. This latter had come in useful when one of the gang brought a calico cat along to the hideout and she would not leave after he grew tired of her. It fell on the two girls to take the errant female out and show her the light.

True, Annie went on, Bill had never yet let them ride on a raid, but she bet he would when she and Britches handed him the ransom money from Mark's father.

They talked on for a time and then Annie rose, walked around the table to sit on Mark's lap and wrap her arms around his neck. She crushed her mouth up to his, kissing him with what she fondly imagined to be more passion than he had ever before come up against in a woman.

"How was that?" she asked, releasing him.

"Not bad at all," Mark replied. "How's about turning me loose so I can sample it properly?"

For a moment he thought she would. Interest, eagerness and anticipation flickered across her face, to be wiped out in an expression of fear almost. She showed the sort of reaction a man on his first visit to a cathouse might have as he approached the door, then saw one of his neighbors coming along the street.

Gently Mark put his hands on her leg and she sprang to her feet, moving hurriedly away from him.

"Oh sure!" she said, breathing heavily. "I unfasten you and the next thing I know is you're headed out of here."

Mark let it go at that. He started to rise and the girl took a hurried pace to the rear. Dropping her hand, she drew the Navy Colt. Mark ignored the move. Turning his back to the girl, he walked across to his bedroll and settled down on it as comfortably as possible to get some sleep.

After a time Mark rolled over and looked to where Annie sat at the table. She had stoked up the stove and range, now she sat with her head rested on her folded arms, fast asleep. Slowly Mark rose, taking up one of his blankets. He went to the girl's side and draped the blanket over her shoulders. Then, grinning to himself, he returned to his bed.

There did not appear to be any point in escaping at the moment, leaving a snug cabin and having to spend the night out on the open range. So Mark went to sleep. One thing he did know. He was not fixing to be around when Bill Doolin came back from the raid and before he left he intended to take a couple of desperate lady outlaws and paddle some sense into their heads, via their seats.

Long practice on trail drives and at other times when setting a watch had been necessary woke Mark. He looked at the clock on the wall, saw it to show time that Britches should take over his "guard." Sitting up he began to cough; it took a few loud barks before Annie opened her eyes and sat up. She threw off the blanket and reached for her gun as Mark rose to his feet.

"Can I go outside?" he asked.

"What for?" Annie snapped.

"Guess."

A slight flush came to Annie's cheeks. She rose, blinking sleepily at the clock, and nodded.

"Go ahead."

"No peeking mind."

When he returned, Mark found a sleepy-looking

Britches emerging from the bedroom, her hair tangled, her shirt half in, half out of her waistband, ankles and feet bare, and carrying her gunbelt in her hand. Flopping in the chair, she dumped her gunbelt on the table.

"You watch him good now, Britches!" Annie ordered.

"I'll do just that," the little girl replied, throwing a suspicious look at the blanket draped over the chair back.

However, once Annie entered the bedroom and settled down Britches rested her head on her plump arms and soon began to bubble gently as she drifted off to sleep. Mark, watching her from his blankets, knew she would make no better a guard than Annie had. Rising, he crossed the room, wrapped the girl up, built up the stove fire without waking either girl, then went back to his bedroll and fell asleep.

The first light of day broke through the window and Mark heard Little Britches stirring. The girl padded across the room to stoke up the stove and range, setting the coffeepot on it. He waited until she had made the coffee before he let her see he was awake.

"Hi!" Britches greeted. "Come on over and drink some coffee."

While drinking the coffee they talked of various things and Mark let slip the information that he knew somebody in whom Britches had a great interest.

"You mean you know Belle Starr?" she gasped.

"Why sure," Mark agreed. "I met her up to Elkhorn three years back."

"You know her *real* well?"

Mark grinned, thinking of his meeting with the famous, or notorious lady outlaw. Anyway a man came to look at it, Mark reckoned he could say he knew Belle Starr *real* well.

"As well as they come, gal," he admitted.

Next moment Britches sat in his lap, her arms around his neck and her mouth thrust to his, kissing him with all the passionate power she could manage. On releasing Mark, Britches stood up, put her hands on her hips, tossed back her head and looked him over in a challenging and provocative manner.

"How does she come up to me?" she asked.

"Nary a comparison, Britches gal."

Fortunately Little Britches took the statement at its face value and did not ask him to explain it further. Britches was a pretty little girl, gay, happy and cute. Yet to compare her with Belle Starr—well it would be like comparing a pretty, friendly, cuddly little house-cat kitten with the latent, wild and savage beauty of a she-cougar.

"Course, a man can't really tell, not unless he's free to get his arms around the gal," Mark went on. "Just cut me loose and we'll try it again."

For an instant much the same expressions played on Little Britches's face as had shown on Annie's when Mark made the suggestion to her. Then Britches winked and bent over, reaching for the rope hobble on Mark's feet. Neither she nor Mark had seen a sleepy-looking Annie emerge from the bedroom and her bare feet made no sound as she crossed the room. Like Britches, Annie had removed her boots and gunbelt before she went to sleep and was not wearing either.

Britches received notice that Annie had woke up when the other girl delivered a roundhouse slap which cracked like a gunshot and landed fairly on the tight stretched seat of Britches's amply filled pants.

"Yeeeow!" Britches yelled, jerking erect and whirling to face Annie. "I was just making sure the rope hadn't slipped."

For all that hot anger flooded her face and tears brimmed in her eyes as she rubbed the spot on which the slap landed.

"Yeah!" Annie replied. "I could see you was."

"Now easy there, Annie," Mark put in. "Tarnation, she kisses just as good as you do."

Instantly the girls were facing each other. Annie opened her mouth to frame an angry, if untrue, denial. She saw the look which came into Britches's eyes and knew she should not have slapped her plump little friend.

Suddenly, without any warning, Britches let Annie have it. Not a slap, but a round-arm punch with her clenched right fist. She swung the blow in the manner Bill Doolin taught her, smashing her fist into Annie's cheek, snapping her head around. At the end of the swing Britches brought the hand whipping back, the knuckles landing on Annie's other cheek and swinging her head over once more.

Mark grunted, wincing in sympathy, for it looked as if Britches knew how to throw a real good punch. With a yell of triumph Britches lunged in, but she was overconfident. Annie, who had staggered back a pace or two, recovered her balance and stabbed a hard right into Britches's plump middle and rocked her back a few steps gasping and holding where the blow landed.

The two girls had always been tomboys and since joining the Doolin gang had received lessons in defending themselves. They appeared to have learned their lessons well. Britches backed off hurriedly, avoiding Annie's rush and keeping her fists raised. Annie shot by Britches, hit the table, which stopped her charge.

Giving a squeal of fury, Annie turned and attacked once more. At the last moment Britches sidestepped and hooked her in the stomach, then clipped her over the ear as she staggered by. Annie hit the wall, twisting around to ram headfirst into Britches's middle and force her backwards. Digging her left hand into Annie's hair, Britches dragged the other girl's head up and started to drive her free fist into Annie's face. Three times she hit, drawing blood from Annie's nose. Then Annie caught Britches by the left wrist, twisted and threw the plump girl over her shoulder. Flinging herself onto Britches, she landed facing the other girl's feet but they rolled and squirmed until they managed to get around and at each other.

Clinging to each other's hair, they rose and reeled across the room. At last Annie forced Britches backwards to hit the table. For a moment Annie held the advantage, yanking at Britches's hair with her left hand, slapping and punching with the right. Desperately Britches wriggled backwards onto the table and Annie followed her. Annie landed between Britches's legs and the little girl wrapped them around the other's slim waist. Crossing her ankles, Britches began to squeeze. From the way Annie howled, Britches's legs packed a fair amount of crushing power.

Squawking in agony, Annie grabbed Britches's hair in both hands, trying to smash her head on the tabletop. One of Britches's wildly flailing hands touched the handle of the coffeepot, missed its hold as her head thudded onto the wood, slapped wildly at Annie's cheek, then came down and caught hold of the handle.

That was when Mark decided to take a hand. The coffee in the pot would be hot enough to give Annie a nasty scald and he knew Britches did not mean to do so, yet in her anger she might.

Lifting his feet, Mark placed them under the edge of the table and tilted it over. The weight of the girls turned the table on its edge and they slid to the floor. Desperately trying to avoid Annie's hands, Britches let the coffeepot fall and it spilled harmlessly onto the floor. Getting her feet under Annie's body, Britches flung the other girl back across the room.

On closing with each other, the girls decided to start using fists again. Annie decided her best hope lay in keeping Britches at range and Mark admired the way the slim girl stabbed out punches which stopped her opponent's rushes and kept her back. For a few seconds she managed to keep it up, then Britches got inside her guard, ripping savage little fists into Annie's ribs. Squealing in pain, Annie trapped Britches's right hand under her arm. Then Annie began to lash her other hand in flat palm slaps and backhand blows across Britches's face.

Britches took it for a moment, then thrust Annie backwards so she crashed into the wall by the door. The impact not only jarred Britches free, but it knocked the catch off the door. Swinging a roundhouse punch, Britches knocked Annie staggering through the now-open door. Lowering her head, Britches charged out after Annie. The thud of a blow sounded and Britches came in again, landing on her plump little rump.

Coming up with a yell, Britches lowered her head to charge into Annie with head down as the other girl appeared in the doorway. They shot through it and out of Mark's sight, but from what he could hear the fight did not slacken its pace any.

Mark had come to his feet after turning the table over. With the girls busy outside, he set the table on its legs again and prepared to escape. Up until the fight started Mark had planned to escape some time in the morning, then take the two girls across his knee and teach them not to waylay and kidnap strangers. From what he had already seen, and from the sounds coming in through the door, Annie and Britches were raising lumps on each other and handing out more punishment than he would have.

Raising his hands, Mark brought them down in the direction of the table. The handcuffs struck the wood and, as he knew they would, burst open. As a trained lawman Mark knew better than leave a handcuffed prisoner unwatched, the girls did not know of the danger.

On the impact, the handcuffs burst open and Mark tossed them aside. His powerful fingers made short work of the hobbles and he rose a free man. Crossing the room, Mark took his gunbelt from the racks and donned it while watching the two girls. They appeared to have forgotten their fistfighting and were rolling over and over in a hair-yanking feminine brawl.

After checking his guns were still loaded, Mark took up his hat, set it at the correct "jack-deuce" angle over his off eye and prepared to deal with the two girls. They seemed to be tempting providence for they had rolled to the edge of the spring and still fought on. Neither had any idea their prisoner had freed himself. Not until they felt a hand clamp on each of their waist belts and lift them into the air.

Although Mark held the squealing, kicking girls in mid-air, they still clung to each other's hair. He swung them forward and sent them flying out over the spring and they disappeared with a splash and muffled, mutual squeals of surprise. They came up spitting water and spluttering. The ducking in the icy cold water appeared to have ended their aggressive desires and they stood hip deep in the spring, side by side looking dazedly around them. It took them almost thirty seconds to realize their prisoner was a prisoner no more and that they were now at his mercy.

"Come on out!" Mark ordered grimly.

Two disheveled girls waded towards him. Both had lost their shirts in the fight; Annie's underskirt had been ripped open but she held it together with both hands; Britches wore a man's undershirt that had been torn across one shoulder and which she held up protectively. Both had a blackened eye, bloody noses and numerous bruises. Alto-

gether they looked like a very sore and sorry brace of
desperate lady outlaws.

Suddenly the life of an outlaw lost its appeal for the two
girls. They found themselves faced with the consequences
of their actions. The man they had so merrily kidnapped
now stood before them and in a position to send them both
to jail for a long time.

Just as they came ashore and started to walk by Mark, a
shot ripped through the air. A second bullet kicked up dirt
between Annie's feet and the third came so close to
Britches it made her yelp in fright and release the vest
which collapsed to expose her chubby, naked torso.

At another time Mark might have enjoyed the view.

"Head for the house!" he ordered.

Neither girl needed twice telling. They had been born
and raised in Indian country and did not need warning
twice when bullets flew. So they took off at a gallop for the
safety of the house.

The shots had come from the corner of the valley. Mark
knew this and he sprang away from the girls, making a fast,
swerving dash towards the slope, hoping to draw the fire
from the girls. He had no idea who the attackers might be,
but he sure as hell did not intend to stop and find out.
Three more shots spattered around him, from two of the
rifles unless he missed his guess, for he had heard another
shot which must have gone in the direction of the girls.

A rolling dive carried Mark to the first of the cover. He
heard the scream of a ricochet as he lit down behind the
rock. Turning, he looked to see how the girls fared. Neither
lay on the ground, which was a relief, and the door to the
cabin slammed even as he looked.

Then Mark turned his attention to his attackers. Two of
them had found a snug spot, one between two large rocks,
the other on the slope side of them. It took Mark just five
seconds to recognize the two flabby hardcases he and
Cousin Beau tangled with in Guthrie. It would appear they
sought revenge.

At that moment Mark remembered the third rifle. Ap-
parently the two men had brought along a friend to even
the odds a mite—or had they come after him at all? Mark
remembered the bartender's pungent comments on how

Rushton and Kinnear made their money. More likely they came after the Doolin gang. Of course the girls would be worthless to the bounty hunters, for they did not have rewards on their heads. However they would know the location of Doolin's hideout, so could lead the bounty hunters to it.

Somehow it did not fit with what he had seen of the two men in town that they would risk tangling with the Doolin gang. Maybe they only hoped to pick off a stray. Perhaps they took him for an outlaw—or they may have recognized him and decided to combine business with pleasure and get their revenge.

Carefully Mark scanned the slope. One thing he did know. He must get in a whole lot closer if he hoped to do any shooting. Maybe if he used both hands, rested his wrists on the rock top and took careful aim he might be able to do something useful at that range. Only while he stayed up there ranging in on the men, they could aim their rifles on him and finish him off, for a rifle was easier to aim over a distance.

With that in mind Mark left his cover and started to move up the steep slope. He wanted to get above the men, always the best place to be in any fight. While not being the Ysabel Kid, who could glide through the thickest cover as silently as a shadow, Mark had taken more than one wary mule deer by stalking it. So he moved from cover to cover, angling up and along the slope.

The man who stalked Mark had Indian blood and knew the secrets of silent movement. Luckily for Mark, the half-breed had never been a very good shot and wanted to get so close he could not miss. Mallalieu's instincts warned him that if his first shot missed, or failed to kill, he would most likely die an instant later. Consequently Mallalieu came to within twenty feet of Mark before he crouched among the bushes and raised his rifle.

In the cabin Britches and Annie, their differences forgotten, knelt by a window, each holding her carbine. From their position they could see the two men by the rocks, Mark moving up and along the slope—and a patch of black where such a color had not been a few seconds before.

"Hold them two down, Britches!" Annie snapped.

Without questioning her friend, Britches started to throw lead at the rocks and her spirited bombardment caused Rushton and Kinnear, never the bravest of men, to duck hurriedly. Annie rested her carbine on the window ledge, took careful aim and fired.

Mark became aware of a smell as he inched along on silent feet. He did not carry his guns in his hands, keeping the hands free for parting branches and giving him support. The smell wafted downwind to him and it took him an instant to recognize it. Then he remembered. The stench of grease-blackened buckskins and stale, unwashed human flesh which often clung to Osage Indian villages. Yet such a smell should not come to him here unless—

Behind the bushes Mallalieu lined his rifle at the big Texan. His finger curled on the trigger, then Annie's bullet slapped the air over his head. He jerked back and his rifle cracked as its muzzle tilted upwards.

Flinging himself to one side, Mark lit down with a gun in either hand. He fired, left, right, left, right, sending the four bullets hammering into the bushes and spacing them along. He heard a gasp and the soggy thud as his fourth bullet struck flesh, so sent a fifth into the same spot. Mallalieu reared upwards into view, his mouth hanging open, a neat hole between his eyes and no back to his head.

Fifteen seconds ticked by slowly. Mark lay under the cover of a rock, his Colts in his hands. He watched the moccasin-clad foot which stuck from behind a bush, but it did not move.

"Looks like he got Sunset," Kinnear remarked, crouching between the rocks and throwing a couple of shots at the cabin.

"Sure," Rushton replied, ducking down as a bullet sent rock chips flying into the air. "But I reckon Sunset downed him at the same time. What now?"

"There's only them two gals and the Texan here. We'll get the gals and make 'em tell us where Doolin and the bunch are. If they haven't pulled the raid, we can telegraph the town they're headed for, warn the marshal and get a cut of the reward."

A loose-lipped, slobbering grin came to Rushton's lips. "We'll do more'n . . ."

Yet the problem of how to get at the girls needed some solving, for both had weapons and showed they knew how to use them. Rushton and Kinnear did not aim to take chances, that had been Mallalieu's side of the partnership, they reserved the safe plays for themselves. Neither man had come up with any startlingly brilliant solution when Mark appeared and took cover behind a huge rock some forty yards above them.

Now Mark also had a problem. A similar problem to the two bounty hunters if he had only known. His problem, like theirs, was how to get close enough to take his opponents without also taking a bullet in the belly.

His eyes checked the area ahead of him. It appeared to have been swept by an avalanche at some time, for it lay more open than most of the slope. Then Mark looked at the rock he stood behind. This rested on a level piece of the slope, but did not appear to be part of it or an outcrop rising above the soil.

Turning, Mark holstered his Colts. He pressed his back against the rock, braced his arms and hands against it, bent his legs and began to push. Never had his enormous strength been put to such a test. Never had so much depended on his muscular powers. Sweat poured down his face, he forced back on the rock, his bootheels gouging into the earth. Joe Gaylin, the El Paso leatherworker who made the boots, always boasted that no power on earth could rip off the heels. Now Mark was giving the boots a thorough test—and they proved Gaylin's boast.

Mark felt the rock move, tilt slightly. He relaxed his hold, seeing that the rock did not settle back again, and turned to look down. Now there was a small gap between the rock and the ground and he knew he could only achieve his aim in one way.

Bending down, Mark put his hands under the edge of the rock, setting his feet a short distance apart and bending his legs. Then he began to lift. Although he felt the tremendous dead weight upon his hands, Mark did not give in. His face twisted from the strain and he felt as if his back would cave in under the weight. Yet he did not give in. Slowly the rock rose and Mark kept up his relentless lifting, moving over a thousand pounds weight by his giant strength.

"Just look at that man!" Britches gasped, forgetting to use her carbine as she watched Mark's efforts.

"Whooee! He makes Bill or any of the boys look like weaklings!" Annie replied, resting her carbine and not firing. "What a man!"

With a final heave, Mark lifted the rock past its point of balance and it started to tilt forward. Mark gave a final thrust and the huge rock turned over, going away from him, bounding and rolling down the slope. Gasping for breath, Mark sank to the ground, but he knew he might still have need to defend himself.

Not until the huge rock began to roll did the two bounty hunters become aware of their danger. The first warning they received came with a dull rumbling sound that drew their attention up the slope. They saw the huge rock rolling, at an ever-increasing speed, down towards their hideout.

Rushton, nearest to the rolling rock, flung himself clear and leapt to safety. Perhaps Kinnear would have been safe in the shelter between the two rocks, but he panicked. Rising hurriedly he tried to dive over the rock on the side away from the rolling menace. His right foot slipped and he fell onto the rock he was trying to climb over. A glance over his shoulder told him he was not going to make it. His scream of terror chopped off in a hideous crunching crash as the huge rock smashed down, coming to rest where Kinnear and his cover had been.

Shaken by the scream, Rushton staggered forward. He still held his rifle and his eyes went up the slope to where Mark stood with hanging head and fighting to recover from his exertion. Throwing up the rifle, Rushton fired a shot at the big Texan, but his nerves had been jolted and he missed. With fumbling fingers Rushton tried to work his rifle's lever.

The bullet missed Mark by inches. It served to warn him of his danger. At that range a man would have to use sights to make a hit and he knew he must hit—or die. He could guess that Annie and Britches would be in no condition to help him after what they must have seen when the rock landed on Kinnear.

Mark's right-hand Colt came from leather and lifted.

Raising the weapon shoulder high, he gripped and supported his right hand with the left, extending his arms almost straight. Sighting the V notch in the tip of the hammer and the foresight, Mark aimed down at Rushton. He fired four shots as fast as he could work back the hammer. The first three bullets missed Rushton, getting closer all the time, as the bounty hunter finished working the lever and sighted again. If the fourth bullet missed, Mark would be a dead man.

It did not miss. Grazing the barrel of the rifle, Mark's .44 bullet whirled off in the buzz-saw action of a ricochet to strike full into the center of Rushton's forehead. It threw him backwards from his feet, his rifle firing off one wild shot as it fell from his lifeless hand.

Like the circuit-riding preacher used to say: he who lives by the gun shall die with lead in his hide. Rushton had killed five men in cold blood for the bounty on their heads. He would never kill again.

Holstering his gun, Mark walked slowly down the slope. He saw the cabin door burst open and waved the girls back inside. Kinnear's body under the huge rock was no sight for a girl to see, even if she was a tough lady outlaw.

Mark counted off a thousand dollars from his wallet and handed it to Cattle Annie.

"Here," he said, "I'm in a hurry to get back to the O.D. Connected. So I'll pay you the ransom and save you holding me until pappy gets up here."

The girls, both wearing new shirts and cleaned up—though showing marks of their fight—stared at the money, then at the big blond Texan. He had buried the two dead bounty hunters and done what he could about hiding all that remained in sight of the third. Now he was preparing to resume his interrupted journey.

"You don't have to give us this," Annie objected and Britches nodded in agreement, their earlier rivalry forgotten.

"Sure I do," Mark replied. "Business is business. Whyn't you girls go off and spend it someplace far from here?"

"That wouldn't be fair to the boys," Britches explained.

"It sure wouldn't," Annie agreed.

Mark shrugged. He knew he could not persuade the girls to change their way of life. Still they seemed happy in it and he reckoned Bill Doolin would see nothing serious happened to them. Swinging afork his blood bay, Mark raised his hat to the girls.

"If I'm ever up this way again, I'll look you up," he promised. *"Adios."*

Standing side by side, their arms around each other's waists, Cattle Annie and Little Britches watched Mark riding south. The little girl sighed and turned to her friend.

"Did he—last night—you know—did he?"

For a moment Annie thought of lying. Then she shook her head.

"No," she said, sounding a little regretful. "How about you?"

"Me neither," Britches confessed just a shade wistfully. "Do you think he knows that we've—that we're—"

"How could he?"

But Mark did know. Which was one of the reasons he had not accepted their invitation to stay on for another night. Which was also the reason why he aimed to steer clear of Cattle Annie and Little Britches—well, at least until they got to be a few years older.